SAWYER

Maddox BRAVO Series

LOGAN CHANCE

Copyright © 2025 by Logan Chance

All rights reserved.

No part of this book may be reproduced in any form or by any electronic or mechanical means, including information storage and retrieval systems, without written permission from the author, except for the use of brief quotations in a book review.

Cover Design by Kim Lehnhardt with Designs With Kimistry

Page edge designs by Painted Wings Publishing

For my Greedy Girls—Kim L., Valerie, Lorey, Kim S., Tiffany, Rochelle, Maria, Kim G., Stacey, Lisa H., Kasey, Lisa A., Maritza, Amy, Julie, Shaunna, Leticia, and Amy W.

If you only read the books that everyone else is reading, you can only think what everyone else is thinking.

Haruki Murakami

The Maddox BRAVO Team

Meet the men and women of the Maddox BRAVO Team founded by Dean Maddox (you can read his story in Stolen By The Boss)

You can grab TONS of bonus content about the Men of Maddox Security over on my Patreon! Character interviews, bonus epilogues, bonus stories, case files, and so much more. CLICK HERE to check it out!

Sawyer Maddox (Dean's cousin), BRAVO's principal-protection lead and resident "walk into the ticking room" specialist. Former military EOD with a planner's brain and a brawler's calm, he builds layered security the way architects pour foundations—advance work, route matrices, de-escalation first, decisive force when it counts. Dry-witted, unflinchingly loyal, and meticulous to a fault, Sawyer counts exits on reflex, keeps a battered field notebook of

The Maddox BRAVO Team

names and verbs, and carries a low-vis kit (SIG, slim carbine, multitool, Faraday pouch) even in a tux.

Andy 'RIGGS' Riggs, BRAVO's resident battering ram with a tactician's brain—broad-shouldered, bearded, and quiet until it's time to breach. He's all steel under pressure, deadpan humor and zero patience for theatrics, but softens for kids, dogs, and the few people he lets inside his circle. Loyal to a fault, he's the man you want at your six when doors—and plans—start to fail.

Gunner Slade, BRAVO's long-range overwatch—quiet as a held breath, deadly precise, and unflappable when the world tilts. A former scout sniper with a side obsession for ballistics and wind charts, he can read a skyline like a map and thread a needle from half a mile. Off-mission he's all dry wit and jazz playlists, flipping a lucky coin he swears only lands heads when the team needs it.

Jaxson Calder, BRAVO's ISR/tech ops specialist. Former USAF pararescue cross-trained in signals intel, he paints the battlespace from three miles up and ghosts enemy comms without leaving fingerprints. Lean, quiet, and razor-focused, Jax flies a fleet of custom micro-UAVs he calls "the choir," hums Motown while jamming signals, and speaks in clean data and drier one-liners. Scar through his right brow, coordinates inked on his forearm (the team's first extraction), and a battered pelican case that never leaves his side. If it's emitting, he's listening—and when Jax is on overwatch, BRAVO moves like it already knows the next five minutes.

Hayes Whitlock, BRAVO's EOD and forensics lead. Former Army bomb tech with two tours disarming IEDs, he's all steady hands and slower-than-your-pulse breathing. Hayes can read a blast scene like a diary—wires, scorch, and shrapnel patterns telling him who built it and where they'll try next. Quiet, dry-witted, and meticulous, he carries a battered toolkit (ceramic blade, non-conductive tape, micro-mirror) and a brass coin he taps once before he cuts. Off-mission he restores vintage watches and spoils the team's K-9 with contraband treats. When Hayes says "slow is smooth," everyone listens—and lives to argue about it later.

About

He's sworn to protect her. She's determined to live her life. Neither planned on falling head-over-body-armor in love.

Heiress Camille "Cam" Kingsley would rather paint landscapes than grace society pages, but someone is sending chilling threats that say Cam's last stroke of the brush should be her last breath. Enter Sawyer Maddox—former Navy EOD tech, fiercely protective, and the newest member of the elite Maddox BRAVO Security Team. His mission: keep the free-spirited heiress alive, even if she believes danger is "just a dramatic misunderstanding."

Sawyer's strategy is simple: lock down the mansion, lock out the bad guys, and absolutely, positively do not lock lips with his client. Easy… until one night when Cam paints for him. With each brushstroke, a blazing fire ignites between them.

With every mischievous grin Cam flashes, Sawyer's bulletproof resolve cracks. And when the threats close in at paint-splattering speed, he'll have to choose between following the BRAVO handbook or following his heart.

Protecting an heiress was never supposed to be this messy. But for Sawyer and Cam, danger might just be the masterpiece that paints them into the greatest love story money can't buy.

1

Sawyer

I'm halfway through dismantling a Glock 19 for a refresher speed-clean when my phone buzzes across the stainless-steel workbench like a restless cricket. One glance at the caller ID—Dean Maddox—and I know break time's over. My cousin doesn't summon me unless something's on fire or about to be.

I pouch the weapon pieces in their velvet slots, wipe my hands, and jog the length of the BRAVO hangar. High above, the company logo—a gold —gleams against charcoal paint. We're supposed to be "private security consultants," but every inch of this place screams paramilitary. There's obstacle courses, target ranges, armored SUVs lined up like obedient rhinos. I love it. After seven years of Navy EOD, disarming bombs, the disciplined hum of ready power is the only lullaby that works on my frayed nerves.

Dean's office sits on a mezzanine overlooking the controlled chaos. Frosted glass, modern lines, basketball-size Himalayan salt lamp that pretends to mask the scent of gun oil. It's a huge step-up from the skyrise he used to conduct business at. This site is more practical.

He's pacing when I step into the large glass conference room we've named the Aquarium. His phone's pressed to his ear, expression welded into that don't-make-me-say-it-twice scowl our mothers swear we inherited from Grandpa Maddox. He jerks a chin at the leather chair opposite his—*sit, stay*—then turns his back and finishes the call.

I sink into the chair. The leather hisses, still warm from whoever just vacated it, and a faint trace of citrus cologne lingers in the air. Something tells me this isn't a routine bodyguard job for a C-list tech bro.

Dean hangs up, pinches the bridge of his nose, and exhales like the world is growing heavier by the minute. "Pack a bag, Sawyer. You deploy in an hour."

I arch a brow. "That's… abrupt. Even for you."

He drops a thick folder onto the desk. Stapled to the cover is a glossy eight-by-ten headshot of *Camille Kingsley*. Even in black-and-white she looks technicolor—wide hazel eyes, bee-stung lips, cheekbones that could slice glass. Her smile is crooked, like she's in on a joke nobody else has heard yet.

"Camille Kingsley," I say aloud, just to make sure the

universe isn't pranking me. "As in Kingsley Aeronautics? The zero-emission jet prototypes?"

"As in *$34-billion market cap*," Dean confirms. "Her father, Gregory Kingsley, is scrambling to finalize an IPO. Two weeks ago Camille started getting threats."

I flip open the folder. Inside: ransom-note letters, photos of bullet holes punched through landscape paintings, a police report stamped *Ongoing Investigation*. My stomach tightens. "The cops have any leads?"

"Nothing actionable. The letters are clean of prints and the phone threats route through VPNs in four continents." Dean plants his fists on the desk. "Gregory's pissed and panicking. He wants BRAVO on Cam twenty-four/seven until the perp is bagged."

"Why me?"

"Because you don't rattle." He slaps my shoulder hard enough to pop a vertebrae. "And because you just finished that cyberstalker case in L.A. without so much as a scratch on the client."

She'd been a Hollywood influencer whose TikTok went feral—easy compare-and-contrast with Camille Kingsley, America's reluctant eco-princess. I've seen Cam's face flash across finance channels and gossip rags: heiress turned rebel artist, paint under her nails instead of champagne bubbles in her flute. I know the basics: refused a seat on the Kingsley board, opened a community art studio in downtown Saint Pierce, donated half her trust-fund allotment to marine-conservation grants. The press either labels her a visionary or a spoiled brat who hates using daddy's jet. Depends which side of the "eat the rich" debate sells more ad space that day.

Dean slides a tablet across the desk. A live security feed fills the screen: Cam's Atlantic Heights mansion—a century-old sandstone beauty that looks like it could outstare Alcatraz. I watch a housekeeper carry tulips through a sunlit foyer. No sign of the princess herself.

"What's the client's attitude toward personal security?" I ask.

Dean snorts. "In her words: 'I'm not running from a boogeyman wearing administrative shoes and a Napoleon complex.'"

I rub my jaw. "Translation: She thinks this is overkill."

"Exactly. Gregory insisted. She tolerated two days with a local outfit before she sent them packing."

"I'll last longer." I grin. "I'm charming."

"You're a bulldozer in combat boots. Just remember she's the job, not the enemy." He tosses me a key fob. "Take Rover Two. It's fully up-armored, fresh from ballistic testing."

I push to my feet. "Any stipulations?"

Sawyer

"Only one." Dean's eyes sharpen. "Keep it quiet. If the press sniffs you, Kingsley stock tanks. That IPO clock's ticking."

Silent and invisible, yeah, I can do that. I've defused warheads behind enemy lines with nothing but a multitool and a prayer. Babysitting one reluctant heiress can't be harder.

TWO HOURS LATER, Rover Two growls up Danforth Street, eating Saint Pierce's asphalt like protein pancakes. Victorian mansions perch on either side, strung with bougainvillea and eight-figure price tags. Camille's address looms ahead—a four-story behemoth fronted by wrought-iron gates tall enough to keep out Godzilla.

The gates swing inward as my SUV approaches. A butler in a crisp white shirt waits at the circular drive, expression set to *professionally unflappable*.

I kill the engine and step out.

"Mr. Maddox?" the butler inquires.

"Call me Sawyer." I flash my best trust-me-I'm-fun smile. "And you are?"

"Edgar, sir. Miss Kingsley is... delayed. She insisted on picking up canvases from her warehouse personally." Edgar's 'professionally unflappable' slips for half a heartbeat and worry flickers behind his eyes. "The driver accompanies her, but I would be grateful for your assessment when she returns."

"I'll take the grand tour." I extend a hand. "Lead the way."

Inside, the mansion is all old-money opulence like coffered ceilings, Persian runners, a chandelier that looks heavy enough to crush the national debt. Yet bright splashes of modern art puncture the traditional decor: neon brush-strokes across antique wainscoting, a bronze sculpture shaped like a melting violin atop a Queen Anne console. Camille's rebellion made manifest.

Edgar points out the obvious weak spots—French windows that date to 1906, two side entrances wired to an alarm system older than me. I nod, and log every detail. Mentally, blueprints bloom like 3-D renders: motion sensors here, pressure pads there, ballistic window film throughout. Forty-eight hours and this place will be Fort Knox wearing a Monet scarf.

We're inspecting the rear terrace when the silence shatters —an engine roars, followed by the crunch of tires over gravel. Edgar exhales a gusty breath. "Miss Kingsley."

Showtime.

I follow him through French doors to the driveway. A vintage red Porsche 356 glides to a stop, chassis coughing like a chain-smoker who's seen better decades. The driver, a lanky kid in a flat cap, leaps out and opens the passenger door.

Camille Kingsley emerges in a swirl of color and chaos. She's barefoot, denim cutoff shorts with turquoise paint-splatters, white tank smeared sunset-pink across her ribs. A loose braid of mahogany hair hangs over one shoulder like the final flourish on an oil-on-canvas masterpiece. Her arms cradle a stack of framed canvases taller than she is; a rogue brush protrudes from behind her ear like a wayward quill.

"What happened to *I just need two*?" the driver groans as he struggles with half the load.

"Creative epiphany happened, Ari." She beams, shifting her burden, and the top frame wobbles, threatening to topple. "Blue period is so last season."

Edgar rushes forward to assist, but Camille steps back, colliding with my chest. A paintbrush spears my collarbone, and lemon aroma fills my lungs. Her shoulder blades are warm through the tank, and I become acutely aware of every weapon currently strapped under my jacket.

"Whoa." Her voice is musical yet husky, like amber whiskey over crushed ice. She pivots, arms still full of canvases, and hits me with those hazel eyes. Up close they're a kaleidoscope—flecks of green, gold, copper—all swirling mischief. "You're not Edgar."

"And you're… heavier than you look." I grip the top canvas, steadying the stack before gravity wins. "Mind if I take a few of these?"

"Please do." She relinquishes half, wiping her forehead with a blot of cerulean that smudges across her brow. "Thanks, uh—?"

"Sawyer Maddox. BRAVO Security." I nod toward the porch, canvases balanced effortlessly. "Your father hired me."

Panic? Fear? Annoyance? I watch her expression like a bomb timer. Instead, she grins—megawatt, unfiltered, dangerously charming. "Dad's being dramatic again. Good luck keeping up, Mr. Maddox."

"It's Sawyer," I correct.

"Fine, Sawyer." She enunciates each syllable like a dare. "But just so you know, I hate the bodyguard vibe. I don't need a shadow. I especially don't need one who wears as much black as a funeral procession."

I glance at my tactical pants and long-sleeve shirt. "Black matches everything."

"So do neutrals." She marches for the door, and I keep pace. Her bare heel brushes my shin once, twice, sending sparks up my thigh. "Let's establish ground rules: no hovering while I paint, no vetoing my schedule, and absolutely no standing outside my bedroom like a gargoyle."

"How about compromise rules? I keep you alive, and you let me do my job."

She opens her mouth—retort locked and loaded—but Edgar interrupts. "Miss Kingsley, perhaps some lemonade first? You've been out all morning."

"And a change of clothes," I add, nodding at the smear of chartreuse across her shoulder. "Paint makes poor body armor."

"Paint is freedom." She winks, handing canvases to Edgar. "But lemonade's a yes. Come on, Sawyer Black-Matches-Everything. Let's debrief."

THE LIBRARY SMELLS like old books and Meyer lemons. Camille flops onto a window seat, crossing paint-stained ankles, while I remain standing—habit born from years spent anticipating mortar rounds. She watches me, eyes narrowing, head tilted like she's figuring out the shading on my silhouette.

"So," she begins, "what's your tactical opinion of my death threat situation?"

"Initial assessment: credible but solvable." I hand her the tablet Dean loaded with the compiled evidence. "Whoever's behind it wants you rattled. The next step is escalation

—something public, something that forces your father's hand."

"Lovely." She scrolls, unimpressed, then freezes on a photo: a Polaroid of her latest gallery show, bullet hole dead-center through the frame. "They ruined *Tempest Horizon*. Took me a month to paint."

"Canvases can be repainted. People can't."

She chews her lip—a soft, plush movement that stirs heat in my chest—and closes the tablet. "All right, Soldier Boy. You're in charge. Where do we start?"

"Full audit of the estate. Then we examine your daily routines—"

"Let me stop you there." She uncrosses her legs, leans forward, elbows on knees. "Tomorrow I'm hosting an art workshop for underfunded schoolteachers. Then, the next day with twenty kids. We're painting a mural downtown."

"I'll scout the site tonight."

"And I'm attending the Kingsley Foundation gala Saturday. Approximately six hundred of my father's closest rich friends."

"I'll coordinate with venue security. You'll have discreet coverage."

"Discreet coverage," she echoes, rolling the phrase across

her tongue like salted caramel. "You really think you can fade into the background?"

"I'm stealthier than you think."

She sweeps her gaze from my broad shoulders to my combat boots. "We'll see."

The air tightens, a taut wire between us. Camille's eyes soften, curiosity blooming. "You always this wound-tight, Sawyer?"

"Occupational hazard."

"Maybe we should loosen you up." She pushes to her feet, toes flexing against Persian weave, and steps into my space—close enough that her lemon-and-turpentine scent tangles with my cedar soap. I tower over her, but she doesn't retreat. Instead, she slides her dry paint-smeared hand around the neckline of my shirt, thumb brushing the hidden mic clipped to the collar.

"Fancy," she murmurs. "Do you record everything your clients say?"

"No mic," I lie, because now I'm conscious of her pulse fluttering beneath turquoise smudges. "Just a button."

"Shame." She flicks the 'button' and steps back, grin turning sly. "Would've made a great art piece: *Surveillance Heartbeat*."

"And what would mine look like?"

"Fast." Her voice drops. "Very fast."

She's not wrong. My heartbeat is hammering like a jackhammer in a quiet chapel. Professionalism fists my collar, drags me upright. "Edgar mentioned lemonade?"

"Kitchen's this way." She twirls, braid swinging, and heads down a corridor lined with abstract seascapes. I follow, chastising my adrenal glands. She's the client. Hands off. Eyes forward. Brain in charge.

Halfway down the hall, a small envelope lies on the floor—plain cream cardstock, addressed in block letters: **CAMILLE.**

She bends to pick it up, but I'm faster. "Allow me." I slip on nitrile gloves from my back pocket before handling the envelope. No postmark, no return address, but the hairs on my neck salute. "Where'd this come from?"

Cam's playful expression melts. "It wasn't here earlier. I swear."

"We'll let forensics decide." I bag the envelope, already dialing Dean. It bothers me that somebody left this right here in her house. Security's shit. I open the envelope, reading the message inside, '*Die, bitch.*'

I don't let her see the message, but my radar kicks to high alert. "Nobody saw anything? Edgar? Anyone?"

"Nobody ever does."

This pisses me off, and I square my shoulders, looking her straight in the eyes. "You don't go anywhere alone."

Her shoulders square, chin lifts. She's about to protest, I can see it, but she swallows the retort. "Okay, Sawyer. I'll listen."

My surprise must show because she laughs softly. "Don't look so shocked. I may be stubborn, but I'm not stupid."

"Smart's good," I say, holstering my phone. "Smart keeps you breathing."

"And stubborn?"

"Stubborn keeps me busy."

Her smile—equal parts gratitude and challenge—fills the corridor with warm light. "Busy isn't always bad."

We resume our trek to the kitchen, but the dynamic has shifted. She lets me walk half a step ahead, yet her presence feels like a current licking my shoulders. This job just morphed from routine to personal, and my instincts buzz with more than protective zeal.

Cam sidles up as we reach the archway. "One more rule, Sawyer."

"Let's hear it."

"No calling me Miss Kingsley unless you're mad at me. It's *Cam*."

"Cam," I repeat, tasting the single syllable, how it hums between us like a live wire.

She pats my chest—right over my heart—and the pink paint smear transfers to my shirt. "Good boy." She winks. "Now about that lemonade…"

I watch her disappear into sun-drenched tiles, and the slap of her bare feet echoes against my ribs. Paint on my shirt, adrenaline in my veins, a mystery envelope in my pocket. This case is going to be hell on my composure—and I'm not entirely sure I mind.

After all, I did promise Dean I don't rattle.

But standing in Camille Kingsley's wake, heartbeat drumming double-time, I realize something else: bombs are simple. *It's masterpieces that are unpredictable—and infinitely more dangerous.*

And I'm already in the splash zone.

2

Camille

I sip lemonade slowly, savoring the tart-sweet burst on my tongue, trying not to notice how my heartbeat hasn't quite settled since Sawyer Maddox walked into my life with his rugged charm and bulletproof everything. Sawyer's presence fills the entire kitchen. The man is a solid wall of muscle, dressed in dark tactical gear that outlines every broad, chiseled plane of his body.

He stands at the kitchen island, examining that cursed envelope he confiscated in the hallway. His brow is furrowed in concentration, the deep lines emphasizing his seriousness. I can't help but find his intensity fascinating, even if it represents everything I've fought to escape—control, limitations, rules.

"You're staring," he says without looking up, his voice smooth with just enough gravel to make my skin prickle.

"I'm observing," I correct lightly. "There's a difference."

He lifts his gaze, and the intensity in his eyes momentarily steals my breath. "And what have you observed so far?"

"You don't trust easily," I answer, setting my glass down carefully. "And you take yourself very seriously."

A slow smirk tilts his lips, transforming his stoic expression into something mischievous and surprisingly enticing. "Is that a bad thing?"

"Depends on the context," I say, matching his playful tone. "Are you this serious all the time, or only when you're saving damsels in distress?"

"You don't strike me as a damsel," he replies smoothly, his gaze dipping just a fraction, enough to send warmth skimming along my skin. "More like trouble wrapped in paint-splattered denim."

I chuckle, leaning against the counter, my fingers tracing idle patterns through a scattering of spilled sugar granules. "Maybe you're smarter than you look, Mr. Maddox."

"Careful," he warns, eyes sparkling. "Underestimating me would be a mistake."

"I'd never." I shake my head dramatically, enjoying our little banter more than I should. "Underestimating you sounds like a dangerous game."

Sawyer

"Yet you don't seem scared," he points out softly, stepping closer, his voice lowering to an almost intimate level. The air between us grows heavy, electric, charged with possibilities I shouldn't even be considering.

"I don't scare easily," I whisper, chin lifted defiantly.

He leans slightly closer, the scent of cedar and clean linen wrapping around me. "Maybe you should."

Before I can reply, Edgar clears his throat loudly from the doorway, and I quickly straighten. Sawyer retreats to a respectful distance, though the intensity of his gaze never wavers.

"Miss Kingsley," Edgar says, eyes darting between us. "Mr. Maddox, Detective Hartley is here."

Sawyer straightens instantly, slipping back into professional mode. "Good. Let's get this envelope to him."

I follow Sawyer out to the foyer, where Detective Hartley stands, looking grim and official as always. Middle-aged with a graying buzz cut, he nods politely at me.

"Camille, sorry we're meeting under these circumstances again."

"Again being the key word," I reply dryly. "You must be tired of my drama by now."

"Never tired of keeping people safe," he says earnestly,

17

taking the bagged envelope Sawyer hands him. "We'll run prints, check for DNA. Hopefully, we'll catch a break."

Sawyer crosses his arms, his biceps straining deliciously beneath the fabric. "Any progress on your end?"

Hartley shakes his head. "No solid leads yet, but we're watching closely. Miss Kingsley, please remain vigilant."

Sawyer glances at me sharply, clearly translating 'remain vigilant' as 'follow Sawyer's orders without question.' I offer a small salute. "Vigilant is my new middle name."

Hartley gives a small smile, handing Sawyer his card. "Call me if anything changes."

Once the detective leaves, Sawyer turns to me, expression steely. "How often do these letters come?"

I shrug, uncomfortable with the direction this conversation is taking. "Every few days, I guess."

"You guess?" His tone hardens. "You need to take this seriously, Cam. Whoever this is, they're escalating. They want something, and they're not going to stop until they get it."

"I am serious," I argue, a stubborn edge creeping into my voice. "But hiding away won't solve anything."

"Neither will pretending it's not happening." He steps closer again, crowding my space, his eyes locked fiercely onto mine. "I can't protect you if you keep acting like you're invincible."

My heart races under the heat of his stare, my breath catching slightly. "Maybe I don't want to feel like I need protection."

"You do," he says quietly, firmly. "And you have it, whether you want it or not."

We stand there, locked in a silent standoff, neither willing to back down. Finally, I sigh, relenting slightly. "Okay, I'll listen. But you have to understand—I won't stop living my life."

"Fair enough," he agrees after a beat. "Then we compromise. You keep me informed, and I'll keep you safe."

"Deal." I hold out my hand, surprised by the strength and warmth of his grip as we shake.

I pull away, suddenly needing air, distance. "Well, Mr. Maddox, if you're planning to shadow my every move, I suggest you become familiar with my home studio. We have a mural to paint Saturday."

"Lead the way." His eyes soften, the intensity replaced by gentle amusement. "And remember, it's Sawyer."

"Right," I say, smiling despite myself. "Sawyer."

I head toward the side exit, feeling his presence behind me like a comforting shadow. We walk out into the sunlight, the lush gardens blooming vibrantly around us, the sweet scent of honeysuckle heavy in the air.

"My studio's back here," I explain, navigating the familiar cobblestone path. "It's my sanctuary."

He makes a soft, approving sound as he steps into my brightly lit haven. Paintings cover every surface—landscapes, abstract shapes, vibrant portraits. Sawyer stops to examine one canvas closely, head tilted curiously.

"Wow," he whispers softly.

I approach, heart fluttering strangely at the vulnerability of sharing this space with him. "What do you think?"

He looks at me, admiration mingling with something deeper, more intense. "Beautiful. Complicated. Like their creator."

My cheeks heat, but I hold his gaze. "Flattery won't earn you points."

"Not flattery," he says quietly. "Honesty."

The air between us thickens once more, pulling me closer to him until I can almost feel the warmth of his body through the small space between us. Sawyer's eyes drop to my lips, and my pulse thunders in response.

Just as I think he might actually lean in and kiss me, a sudden sharp sound shatters the moment—glass breaking, coming from somewhere outside.

Sawyer's stance shifts instantly, his body shielding mine protectively. "Stay here."

Sawyer

Heart pounding wildly, I watch him stride swiftly toward the sound, hand already at his side, ready. I'm left standing there, breathless, terrified, and undeniably exhilarated by the protective force that is Sawyer Maddox.

I already know he's trouble. The best kind.

3

Sawyer

The night air smells like jasmine and damp stone as I step onto the veranda, eyes sweeping left to right, corners first —hedge line, gate, dark windows. A stray bottle rolls along the flagstones, clinking once before settling against the step —teenagers' litter kicked loose by the wind, nothing more. My pulse eases a notch. I pick it up, drop it in the bin, and stand a beat longer under the quiet, letting the house's breathing sync with mine before I go back inside.

I head back inside to watch her paint. Her eyes clock mine as I step back inside the studio, and I nod, letting her know the threat is all clear.

She releases a breath, and returns to her canvas.

Camille paints like she breathes. Recklessly. Gloriously. And without apology. The afternoon light knifes through the clerestory windows of her studio, scattering rainbows across turpentine-speckled drop cloths and kissing the warm tan of her shoulders. She's barefoot again, toes flexing against the splattered floorboards, hips swaying in a rhythm that has nothing to do with music and everything to do with instinct.

I station myself at the edge of the room, just close enough to intercept trouble, far enough to pretend I'm not cataloging every flex of her calf as she stretches for a stroke of cobalt. The SIG at my hip feels suddenly crude, a metal anachronism in a temple of color. Cam doesn't acknowledge me at first. She's lost to the canvas, wielding a three-inch brush like a saber, slashing oceans of indigo into existence.

"Background first," she murmurs to herself. "Foundation before crescendo."

The words aren't meant for me, but they land anyway—an artist's version of battlefield doctrine. Build the groundwork, then add the fireworks. I fold my arms, leaning against a beam, and let my pulse slow. There's something almost obscene about the intimacy of watching someone create. It's like spying on prayer.

Cam steps back, smudges a line with her thumb, leaves a streak of cerulean on her skin. Every few minutes she dips her brush into murky water, splatters droplets on her thigh, then attacks the canvas again. Flashes of sun ignite in her braid, and I catch myself wondering how that hair would feel wrapped around my fingers.

Focus, Maddox.

I do a slow visual sweep: three windows, all original brass latches—no forced entry marks. Door behind me, wide open; good sight lines. Overhead vent big enough for a raccoon, not a perp. No hidden drones, no fiber-optic camera lenses glinting in the rafters. Still, someone breached *somewhere* to plant that envelope. The question scribbles itself across my brain: *How?*

Cam finally notices me hovering. She dabs her brush in yellow, cocks her head. "You're wound tighter than a drum. Does the color help or make it worse?"

"Depends," I answer. "Do you have industrial-grade drop cloths for my anxiety?"

She laughs, the sound sliding under my ribs. "Come here."

I straighten. "Excuse me?"

"Not to model. Relax." She points at the unpainted corner of the mural. "Hold this palette while I finish the horizon line. Trust me, it's easier than juggling it myself."

Everything in the BRAVO handbook screams about maintaining a tactical bubble, but her eyes sparkle with challenge, and I can't resist. I step forward, take the wooden palette—heavy, cool, alive with scent of oils. She brushes past me to reach her mark; the side of her breast grazes my forearm through the thin cotton of her tank. A hit of electricity detonates low in my gut.

Sawyer

Steady, soldier.

She paints, and I play human easel, watching veins of amber swirl into the indigo, watching her lips purse in concentration. At one point she lifts the palette with both hands to mix, and paint smears the back of my knuckles, a vivid poppy red. She catches the gesture, meets my eyes. Chemistry snaps taut between us like a tripwire.

"Told you painting was messy," she whispers.

Messy. Dangerous. Addicting.

Before I can reply, my phone buzzes. It's the BRAVO secure channel. Wicked timing. I swipe the screen one-handed.

"Sawyer here," I mutter, turning away. "Talk."

"Got the first pass on that envelope from the detective," Riggs says. "No prints, but the paper stock is specialty—Arcana Ivory, sold to exactly eleven boutiques in the Saint Pierce area. I'm sending the list."

"Run surveillance pulls near all eleven in the last month. Flag anyone following Cam or Kingsley family staff."

"On it."

I hang up, catch Cam's curious look over her shoulder.

"Work?" she asks.

"Clues."

She bites her lip, studying me, then goes back to the canvas. Ten minutes later she steps away, satisfied. The horizon glows like molten honey. The room smells of pine solvent and electric tension.

"Moment of truth," she says, turning. "Verdict?"

"It looks like the sunset over a war zone," I answer honestly. "Devastating and hopeful at the same time."

Her cheeks flush. "Not everyone sees both."

"I've seen worse skies." My voice dips, remembering sandstorms smeared with tracer fire. "Yours ends with light."

She opens her mouth, maybe to thank me, maybe to flirt, when Edgar interrupts with the dinner gong—yes, a literal bronze gong. Money, apparently, buys medieval theatrics. Cam rolls her eyes. "If I don't show, Edgar will organize a search party. You coming?"

"I'll roam the perimeter first," I answer. "Meet you there."

She nods as she slips from the studio. I wait until her footsteps fade, then swipe a quick UV scan wand along the doorframe—no residue, no hidden microdots. Still, my gut says the breach was inside, not out. Trust but verify. Mostly verify.

Dinner happens in a dining hall big enough to host NATO talks. It's just Cam, me, Edgar, and two silent maids who materialize courses like stagehands. Cam sits at the head. I sit on her right. She attempts small talk—art, weather, an upcoming charity gala—but every clink of silver jolts my hypervigilance.

After dessert—an obscenely decadent lavender crème brûlée—Cam pushes back her chair. "Come on, Maddox. Time to pick your sleeping quarters."

Edgar bristles. "I would be happy to—"

"I've got it," she insists, and I follow her up the sweeping staircase.

She stops at a mahogany door halfway down the east wing. "You'll stay here." She opens to reveal a suite that could house a minor royal. It's got a king bed, marble bathroom, and a balcony facing the ocean.

"Appreciated," I say, scanning angles. Closets deep enough to hide a linebacker. Windows double-latched, but the balcony rail is only seven feet from a drainpipe—note to self: install motion sensors.

"My room's two doors down," she offers, voice husky with something unnamed. "In case you need me."

"I'll manage." My tone comes out rougher than intended.

Her smile is Cheshire-cat slow. "Sleep well, Sawyer." She pivots, her braid sliding across her spine, and she disappears into the dim hall.

I DO NOT SLEEP WELL.

2300 hours: I lie flat on five-hundred-thread-count sheets staring at the ornate ceiling medallion. The house groans like an old ship. Every pop of timber sounds like a footstep. I replay the timeline: envelope found at sixteen-twelve. Staff accounted for. Windows locked. Front gate monitored. So how did the perp get in? Drone drop? Unlikely—no open skylights. Insider? More likely. Could be a disgruntled employee, a contractor with a grudge, a social engineer who sweet-talked delivery access.

2330: I give up, grab my phone, dial Dean.

"Status?" he answers, with no preamble whatsoever.

"Something's off," I say, keeping my voice low. "Perp left an envelope inside a secure perimeter. No breach signs. Paper stock exclusive."

"Inside job," Dean concludes. "Want me to run backgrounds on staff?"

"Edgar's been with the family twenty years, the maids longer. But yes. And check any recent contractors: HVAC, painters, IT."

"Copy. Anything else?"

I hesitate. "Cam's resisting lockdown. She's… spirited."

Dean chuckles. "And you like spirited."

"This isn't about me."

"Sure it isn't. Stay sharp. Call if you need backup." He hangs up.

I scrub a hand over my face, push off the bed. Sleep later. Secure now.

0120 hours: The corridor is dark, lit only by wall sconces casting amber pools across Persian rugs. I sweep left to right: thermal monocular up, scanning for heat signatures. Cam's door glows warm through oak—she's alive, maybe dreaming of sunsets and rebellion.

I move to the south wing of the library—windows locked. Dining hall—empty. Kitchen—empty.

Past the butler's pantry, I find a servant stairwell spiraling to the basement. Door is ajar. My pulse spikes. I draw the SIG, thumb the flashlight, and descend silently.

Basement smells of earth and vintage wine. Racks line the walls, shadows deep as coffins. A faint breeze brushes my cheek—not possible in a sealed cellar. I follow it to a narrow service tunnel, brick arching overhead.

There: fresh scuff marks on the dust. Recent. Size eleven boot, non-dress tread. Adrenaline crashes my bloodstream.

The tunnel ends at a steel access hatch. It's latched from the inside. I crack it open, flashlight slicing darkness. Outside: the rear hedge, thirty yards from the house. A perfect insertion route for someone who knows the layout.

But that means whoever dropped the envelope had interior knowledge and a key—or help.

I secure the hatch, triple knot a length of paracord through the interior lock, and cinch it tight. That hole is plugged.

Back upstairs, I log findings, set extra cameras on the east wing, then stop outside Cam's door, listening. Soft music filters through—jazz, slow and sultry. I imagine her curled under silk, lashes fanning her pink cheeks, unaware of the storm gathering.

I turn away. Protect, don't covet.

0345 hours: I'm on the balcony outside my room, the moon lighting up the ocean waves. The night is cool, salt tang on the air. Somewhere inside, an antique clock chimes four. Footsteps approach—bare and light.

I pivot. Cam stands in the doorway of my balcony, robe cinched, braid loose, eyes drowsy. "Couldn't sleep?" she whispers.

"Patrol." I nod toward the grounds. "Secured a vulnerability."

She hugs herself against the chill. "You're relentless."

"Occupational hazard."

She steps closer until the moon outlines her face. She's luminous. "Thank you," she says simply.

"For?"

Sawyer

"Caring whether I wake up tomorrow." Her hand lifts, and brushes the sleeve of my shirt as it lingers. Heat blooms.

"I'd like you to wake up every tomorrow," I admit.

Silence stretches. Her gaze drifts to my mouth; mine to hers. The world narrows to the silver flecks in her irises, the cinnamon scent of her skin.

I step back. "Go inside, Cam. Get some rest."

She studies me a beat longer, then nods. "Good night, Sawyer."

"Night."

She slips away.

I exhale the breath I didn't know I held, then key the radio to silent mode. One more sweep before dawn. Whoever's hunting Camille Kingsley has no idea the predator now guarding her door is hungrier than they are.

Let them come.

By the time the first blush of sunrise bleeds over the ridge, I'm still awake—wired, focused, and unwilling to admit that the real reason sleep eludes me is a barefoot artist with paint under her nails and the power to redraw every line I thought I'd etched in stone.

4

Camille

The morning sun pours molten gold across my bedroom ceiling, but it's Sawyer's knock—precisely 07:00—that drags me from a tangle of linen and half-remembered dreams. I expected him, however still, the punctuality is almost comical. My guardian gargoyle runs on military time and roasted coffee.

"I'll be five minutes," I call through the door, hopping into linen pants splattered with last night's cobalt.

"You said that ten minutes ago," he rumbles back—amusement threaded through the warning.

I crack the door, toothbrush jutting from foamy lips. "Creative types can't be rushed."

"Security protocols can." He thrusts a travel mug my way. "Lemon ginger tea. Edgar swears by it."

Sawyer

The gesture tugs a smile from my sleepy face. "You bribed Edgar for intel?"

"I might have." His eyes sweep the room behind me, already cataloging threats that don't exist. "Three minutes, Cam."

We're in his Range Rover by 07:30, barreling toward Mission Heights Elementary—one of those turn-of-the-century brick fortresses saved from demolition by a coalition of stubborn parents and crowdfunded miracles. The district cut arts funding years ago. Today's workshop keeps creativity alive on a shoestring and a prayer.

Sawyer drives, posture textbook perfect. His black polo strains across shoulders sculpted by sins I'm willing to confess later. He scans each intersection, eyes flicking like chess pieces.

"Relax," I tease, propping paint-stained sneakers on the dash. "We're headed to finger-paint central, not a war zone."

"Complacency is the real war zone," he counters, but those glacier-gray eyes warm around the edges.

I study him while he studies everything else—the faint scar at his brow, the disciplined set of his jaw, the way his right index taps the steering wheel every seven seconds exactly. A metronome disguised as a man.

"You tap when you're thinking," I observe.

He arches a brow. "You clocked the timing?"

"Artists notice rhythm."

A corner of his mouth curves, as if he's surprised by the fact that he's smiling.

Mission Heights bristles with morning energy—teachers corralling coffee, kids in neon sneakers, the custodian singing Motown under his breath. Sawyer sweeps ahead of me, ID badge clipped to his belt. He checks perimeter doors, bathroom windows, even peeks behind a stack of janitorial bins. It should annoy me, but watching that precision in motion is… distracting.

"Clear," he announces after fifteen minutes, rejoining me outside Room 12—ART LAB stencilled crookedly on peeling paint.

Inside, twenty teachers wait at battered plywood tables. Mason jars overflow with brushes; recycled yogurt tubs brim with cheap acrylics. Sunlight spills through high windows, dust motes dancing like lazy confetti.

"Morning, everyone!" I clap, electricity zipping through me the way it always does before I throw a party on canvas. "Today we're exploring under-painting and glazing—think of it as the secret love affair beneath every masterpiece."

A ripple of excited chatter. I introduce Sawyer—"extra set of hands, makes a mean security perimeter"—and field the predictable jokes about bodyguards and dangerous easels.

He acknowledges them with a dip of his head, eyes already mapping exits.

We dive in. I demonstrate layering burnt sienna beneath translucent ultramarine to birth impossible purples. The teachers—my people—laugh when my hands fly, gasp when pigment blooms across wet paper like living flame. And always, always, I feel Sawyer's gaze: steady, supportive, searing imagination into the small of my back.

At one point I ask for a volunteer. Becca Ortiz—fifth-grade math teacher and resident ray of sunshine—bounces forward. I guide her stroke by stroke, hand over hand. When she catches Sawyer watching, she fans herself theatrically.

"Cam," she stage-whispers, "if security detail looks like that, sign me up for witness protection."

The room erupts with giggles. My cheeks burn hotter than cadmium red, but I keep my tone breezy. "He's strictly professional, Bec."

"Professionally gorgeous," she mutters, returning to her seat.

I pretend concentration, though heat coils low in my belly. Yes, Sawyer is gorgeous. And yes, the way his eyes follow me—not possessive, but aware—is doing scandalous things to my focus.

Two hours flash by in a technicolor blur. Finished pieces dry on makeshift clotheslines, shivering like prayer flags. The teachers hug me, promising to use the techniques in class. Becca lingers.

"So, Sawyer," she says coyly, extending a paint-stained hand. "Any chance you moonlight as a model?"

His lips twitch. "No ma'am. Strictly in the protection business."

"Pity." She winks at me. "Cam, guard that one. He's lethal."

I manage a laugh, nudging her toward the exit. "See you soon, Bec."

Once the last teacher filters out, I start cleaning brushes. Sawyer appears at my elbow, rolling up his sleeves, and *holy arm porn*. His forearms should be illegal. "Let me."

I watch muscles flex beneath tanned forearms as he swirls sable bristles through jar after jar. "Didn't know bodyguards came with art-cleaning abilities."

He glances sideways. "We adapt."

"Always adapting," I echo softly, aware how close his hip is to mine. Static arcs between us, a live wire just begging to be touched.

The custodian coughs from the doorway, breaking whatever spell forms over soap-suds. Sawyer stiffens, professionalism snapping back into place.

"Time to roll," he murmurs.

THE DRIVE HOME coils with thick silence. The sun beats on the windshield. Sawyer's sunglasses hide his eyes, but I feel them anyway. Halfway across the Saint Pierce Bridge, I risk a look. His grip on the wheel is white-knuckled.

"You okay?" I ask.

"Thinking," he replies.

"Dangerous habit."

That earns a ghost of a smile. "Just replaying entry points. The school felt safe, but complacency—"

"—is the real war zone. I remember." I nudge his arm with mine, teasing. "Guess I should be flattered you stayed glued to my six."

He shifts in the seat, tension crackling. "Wasn't exactly a hardship."

I bite the inside of my cheek to keep from grinning like a lovesick teen.

Back at the estate, late-afternoon light drapes the facade in rose-gold. Edgar greets us with news of fresh-baked focaccia. I intend to shower first, but Sawyer places a gentle hand on my elbow.

"Walk with me. Five minutes."

I follow him through French doors onto the west terrace. The garden sprawls: wisteria, fountain, ivy climbing marble columns. He stops beneath a willow, where dappled shade paints stripes across his jaw.

"What's wrong?" I ask.

"Nothing's wrong." His voice is low, sandpaper-soft. "Just needed a breath before we dive back into fortress mode."

My pulse skitters. We stand inches apart—close enough to feel the warmth radiating off his chest.

"Cam," he says, sweeping a stray hair from my face, fingers lingering at my temple, "today at the school… I realized I can't guard you if I'm distracted."

"Distracted how?" The question flutters from my lips like a dare.

"By this." His hand slides to cradle my jaw, thumb tracing the bow of my mouth. Electricity detonates behind my ribs.

"And what is 'this,' exactly?" I breathe.

"A tactical nightmare." He leans in until his breath ghosts across my lips. "And the only thing I've thought about since I met you."

Sawyer

The world narrows to willow rustle and heartbeat thunder. I rise on tiptoe, eyes half-lidded. His fingers tense, as if weighing consequences.

Footsteps crunch on gravel—Edgar, announcing dinner. Sawyer's hand falls away and I swallow disappointment—and relief?—like bitter wine.

He clears his throat. "We should—"

"Yeah." I hug my arms around myself. "Focaccia waits for no one."

We head inside. The charge between us doesn't dissipate. Instead, it coils, simmering, a fuse burning slow. I know two things with blinding clarity: Someone out there wants me afraid—and someone right here makes me feel anything but.

Somehow, I suspect the second danger might be the harder one to survive.

5

Sawyer

I'm pacing the terrace outside the dining room the way most people scroll their phones—endlessly, compulsively—because distance and night air are the only things keeping me from replaying the garden incident on loop. One reckless heartbeat, one brush of hair from Cam's soft skin, and all the protocols I live by crumpled like tissue.

My pulse jolted, and her breath hitched. The sky, already gold with late afternoon, slipped into dusky rose— and I almost did something irreparable.

Almost.

A throat clears behind me. Edgar stands framed in the French doors, silver tray poised like a diplomatic flag.

"Dinner is served, Mr. Maddox."

Showtime. I roll my shoulders, carve professionalism back onto my features, and step inside.

Tonight's meal is seared salmon with citrus couscous—Camille's idea of "light," Edgar's idea of "fussy," my idea of *one more arena where I have to stare at her mouth without acting on impulse.*

She arrives barefoot, a breezy linen dress skimming her knees, auburn braid undone so loose waves tumble over her shoulders. No paint tonight—just dewy skin and those kaleidoscope eyes that see more than they should.

I hold her chair. She thanks me, voice low, and the soft brush of her arm along mine sparks like a live current. We eat, make small talk about tomorrow's mural project. I keep my replies clipped, neutral; she frowns as if she can feel every syllable I swallow instead of speak.

By the time Edgar clears plates, my appetite is as deserted as a demilitarized zone. Cam excuses herself to prep supplies for the morning. I linger at the table, monitoring her retreat down the hall—hips swaying, bare soles whispering over Persian wool—and know I'm teetering on the edge of something no Kevlar can deflect.

I fish out my phone, thumb hovering over Dean's number. *Request reassignment* flickers like an emergency exit sign. It would be the smart move. Smart moves keep assets safe and operators out of headlines. Then a second image pushes in—Camille flanked by some other agent, Riggs or

Jax or maybe even Dean Maddox himself. Someone else shadowing her laughter, someone else catching her when the world turns ugly hell-bent.

Acid churns in my gut. No. I want my hands on this detail —*literally, figuratively,* all of it. If that means I white-knuckle restraint, so be it.

I dial Dean anyway.

He picks up on the third ring, voice gravelly with late-night paperwork and overpriced espresso. "Talk to me."

"Need a second operator tomorrow. Public mural site, twenty minors, open street access on two sides, one service alley in back."

Silence while he scrolls mental rosters. "You requesting Jax?"

"Riggs." The name comes out before I can second-guess it. Riggs is blunt force married to dry wit—and crucially, he'll keep his eyes on threats, not on Cam.

Dean chuckles. "Ah, you want muscle *and* manners."

"I want coverage," I correct, maybe too quickly. "Riggs is local, familiar with SP street grids. Give me the green light and I'll send coordinates."

"You got it. He'll be wheels-up at oh-six, meet you on-site by eight-thirty." Dean's pause lengthens, turns weighted. "Everything else good?"

Sawyer

For a beat I consider telling him—the moment in the garden, the way my pulse recalibrates whenever Cam so much as says my name. Instead I scan the chandelier, assess vantage angles, run threat models—and lie. "All clear," I say.

"Copy. Keep it tight, Sawyer."

We hang up. I clench the phone, thumb barely shy of cracking the screen. *Keep it tight.* Dean has no idea how taut this line is.

Midnight. The mansion yawns with antique echoes while I comb floor by floor, tension coiling tighter than the sling on my sidearm. Third sweep tonight—overkill, but after yesterday's envelope breach I don't trust the estate's perimeters.

Library windows: latched.

Conservatory doors: alarmed.

Studio skylight: new locking pins installed. I hover there a moment, moonlight spilling over half-finished canvases. One bears the new cerulean swipe I added—the tiniest infringement on her art, yet somehow intimate as a fingerprint on skin.

I shove the thought aside, move on.

Upstairs, the hall outside Cam's bedroom glows with a single sconce. I halt, ears filtering for anomaly: HVAC hum, distant surf, nothing else. Good.

Her door is closed, but soft light seeps beneath. She's awake, probably coaxing color palettes or reading dog-eared poetry. I turn away—then stop when floorboards creak behind me. The door cracks open.

She stands in the sliver of light, wearing an oversized Kingsley Aeronautics T-shirt that skims mid-thigh, bare legs pale against the darkness. Sleep-mussed hair frames her face, and her eyes, heavy-lidded, settle on me like a secret invitation.

"Everything okay?" she whispers.

"Routine sweep," I murmur back. My voice shouldn't sound this rough. "Go back to bed."

She opens the door wider, and steps into the hall. "Couldn't sleep?"

"Not a wink." I want to tell her it's the adrenaline, the case, maybe the espresso Edgar thinks I don't sneak at midnight. But we both know what really keeps me wired.

She tosses me a look that reads she's concerned.

"I'm fine, Cam." I force a step back, widening the gap. "Door locked?"

She nods, chewing her bottom lip—the same lip I damn near tasted in the garden. "Tomorrow's a big day," she says softly. "Lots of eyes."

"Nothing we can't handle."

"*We.*" She smiles at that syllable, like it tastes good. Then, gentler: "You'll rest?"

"I'll try," I say, which is the safest form of the truth.

She reaches out—slow, tentative—touches the hem of my T-shirt, just a brush of knuckles. "Goodnight, Soldier Boy."

I step away before I do something catastrophic. "Goodnight, Cam."

She slips back inside, and the latch clicks. I stare at that door exactly three seconds too long, then force myself down the hall, down the stairs, down into the ops room where blueprints wait like cold water.

03:12 hours— my laptop glows with schematics of the Cabana Beach parking lot where the mural project will unfold. I annotate choke points, CCTV blind spots, assign sectors for Riggs. The act of planning is normally balm for my nerves; tonight it's a tourniquet—tight enough to keep blood away from thoughts of Cam curled in bed, T-shirt riding high as dreams drift low.

Focus, Maddox.

I run drills in my head:

08:30—Riggs checks alley, establishes command post by van.

09:00—Cam sets up paint. Kids arrive; parents sign waivers.

09:05—perimeter walk every seven minutes; call signs, comm checks.

Bullet points march into place; order blooms. Underneath, desire thrums—unruly, insurgent. The contrast almost tears me in two.

At 04:45 the sky over the bay bruises lilac. I power down, squeeze the bridge of my nose. Another day starts in ninety minutes, and if I'm lucky I'll snag a twenty-minute combat nap before Cam finds me.

I should be exhausted. Instead I feel blazing, alive, nerve endings humming like live wires. Because I get to guard her again. Not because I'm the only one who can—but because I'm the one who *will*.

And nobody—no stalker, no sniper, no other BRAVO operative—is taking that from me.

6

Camille

Morning smells like espresso, turpentine, and impending trouble.

I'm up before my alarm, jittery with the kind of energy that feels half excitement, half storm warning. Today's the community mural—twenty kids, six teachers, three pallets of paint, and a ridiculously competent security specialist. I tug on ripped jeans I don't mind destroying and a Kingsley Foundation tee, then knot my hair high. I'm swiping an indigo streak across my eyelid (makes hazel eyes pop in photos; sue me) when my phone buzzes.

Sawyer: *Wheels roll in 10. You need protein.*

Me: *Are you my bodyguard or my nutrition coach?*

Sawyer: *Both. Downstairs.*

I grin despite myself.

He's waiting in the kitchen with a travel mug (rocket-fuel latte, vanilla, oat—nailed it again) and a foil-wrapped breakfast burrito I'd normally forget to eat until noon. He doesn't comment when I inhale half of it standing by the island, just hands me a napkin and a tactical vest-shaped fanny pack loaded with hand wipes, mini sunscreen, and a collapsible water bottle.

"You realize this is overkill," I say, wiping salsa from my thumb.

"You say overkill, I say normal." He shoulders a duffel. "Riggs is en route. We'll link up on-site."

"That's the friend you called last night?" I ask, because yes, I heard him in the hall at some inhuman hour, low voice edged in gravel as he spoke to Dean. The walls of this house are thick, but my curiosity is thicker.

"BRAVO teammate," he corrects. "Former Force Recon. Good eyes. Better jokes. Don't let him talk you into parkour."

"Noted."

We take the Foundation van today. Sawyer insisted on swapping out license plates and adding a portable dash cam that feeds straight to his tablet. He drives. I sketch in the air, explaining what the kids will design on the mural today: a river of color pouring out of cracked asphalt, turning into a school of fish that morph into paper airplanes that become ideas that become—"—the city skyline," I finish, air-brushing invisible strokes. "Hope, motion, continuity."

"Symbol heavy," he says, but the corner of his mouth tips. Translation: he likes it.

Traffic crawls through Dansforth Hill, then spits us into Blue-Sand Beach where the old municipal parking wall waits—gray, pitted, a thousand square feet of urban meh begging to be transformed. A nonprofit rec center across the alley is lending us restrooms and storage; the principal already signed waivers, bless her.

An unmarked matte-gray pickup idles across the street. The driver jumps out the second we roll up: tall, rangy, beard like he lost a bet with a lumberjack, mirrored shades. He wears BRAVO cargo pants, a faded baseball cap, and a grin that says *I specialize in trouble, and I'm glad you brought some.*

"Morning, Sunshine," he calls to Sawyer.

"Riggs." Sawyer clasps forearms with him—battle-brother style—then angles toward me. "Cam, meet Andy Riggs, we call him Riggs. He'll be second watch."

Riggs pops the shades up onto his hat and whistles low. "You didn't mention your client was *the* Cam Kingsley. Thought you were dragging me out here for graffiti control." He sticks out his hand, and I like him instantly. "Ma'am."

"Cam," I correct. "Or I'll start calling you Sergeant Beard."

He barks a laugh. "Heard you were mouthy. This is going to be fun."

Sawyer gives him the look—the one that could cauterize a wound at twenty paces. "Focus. Perimeter first."

They fall into a rhythm so practiced it's almost choreographed. Riggs sweeps the rooflines, counting windows. Sawyer maps ingress/egress, chalking colored X's on the ground like he's laying mines. Whatever all of that means. They set up collapsible stanchions to create a kid-safe zone, position the van as a barrier on one end and Riggs' truck on the other, and plug a portable camera into a lamppost. It feels… excessive. Also reassuring, in the way wearing a helmet is annoying until the fall.

"You two guarding paint or the Crown Jewels?" I call.

"Paint *is* the crown," Riggs replies. "Ask Banksy." Then, in a quiet voice to Sawyer, "She's gonna be a handful."

"I heard that," I sing back. "And I'm impressed you know who Banksy is."

Sawyer and Riggs exchange a glare, and I laugh. If I didn't know any better I'd say Sawyer's jealous, and that does something wicked to my body.

I suck in a deep breath.

Sawyer

Kids begin arriving in a noisy trickle—backpacks, lunch sacks, excitement ricocheting off concrete. Becca's here, hair in a high neon scrunchie, arms loaded with dollar-store aprons she insisted she buy when she saw my nicer ones. Principal Nguyen hugs me and introduces parents, all of whom take obvious comfort from the Terminators bracketing the site.

Sawyer crouches to eye level with a trio of second graders. "Rule one: paint the wall, not your friends. Rule two: stay inside the cones unless a grown-up says okay. Rule three: if you need the bathroom, you tell me or Miss Cam." He taps his earpiece. "I can hear everything. Even sneezes."

One kid—Miguel—gasps. "Even burps?"

Sawyer pretends to think. "Especially burps."

The kids lose it, delighted. Becca nudges me. "He has layers. Like lasagna."

"Stop ogling my security," I whisper-laugh.

"Can't. Won't." She winks at me.

We grid the wall in light chalk, then let chaos bloom. Sky blues swish; citrus yellows explode; small hands press stencils; bigger hands roll primer; someone sneezes hot pink. I circulate like a traffic cop with glitter authority, redirecting drips and mediating color disputes ("Yes, the fish can be magenta; no, that doesn't make it less of a fish").

Every time I turn, Sawyer is *there*—not hovering (okay, hovering), but in that elliptical orbit where he can intercept anything headed toward me. When paint water spills, he's got towels. When a gust threatens to flip our supply table, he clamps it with one giant palm. When Miguel's little sister wobbles on a step stool, Sawyer just appears and steadies it, unruffled.

"Captain Serious saved me," she sings to her friends.

"Serious?" Riggs snorts. "Kid, that man once ate a ghost pepper MRE and barely blinked."

"Because my tongue died," Sawyer mutters.

I laugh so hard I bend over, smearing cobalt on my knee.

Riggs soon has a fan club. He teaches the older kids how to mask off sharp lines with painter's tape. "Crisp edges make your colors pop," he says. "Same as keeping your muzzle clean." Blank stares. He amends: "Same as sharpening your colored pencils." Ahh, comprehension.

Lunchtime. The air smells like food truck tacos we bribed a vendor to park nearby. I sit on an upturned milk crate, chewing guac-stuffed something while Sawyer stands, scanning, one hand resting near his hip holster under a loose overshirt. His eyes sweep, sweep, then snag on mine. Heat detonates in my chest. I hold the gaze, and slow-blink once. He exhales, and gives me a lopsided smile.

Sawyer

This man is a walking restraint system, I think. *And every time he locks down, I want to undo a buckle.*

Afternoon light turns syrupy. The mural starts to look like a *thing*—river bursting, fish flowing, paper planes carrying ideas toward a skyline that is, frankly, better than some of the public art commissions the city's approved in the last decade. Kids pose for pics, faces streaked in primary colors. Parents clap. We're down to touch-ups when Principal Nguyen asks if I'll say a few words on camera for the Foundation socials.

"Give me five to de-smurf," I tell her, handing my brush to Becca.

The rec center bathrooms are through a short interior hallway that cuts under the building. Sawyer clocks my trajectory instantly. "Riggs stays here. I'll escort."

I lift a brow. "I can pee without a tactical convoy."

"Humor me."

He walks me to the rec center door, scans inside, then—because kids are lined up at the sinks painting themselves whiskers for TikTok—backs out. "You good?"

"Always."

"Two minutes," he says into his mic. "Eyes on hallway."

I duck inside. The smell hits first: bleach, damp tile, a faint undertone of whatever chemical cocktail public restrooms never fully remove. I pick the last stall, splatter a paper towel with water and dab at my face, elbow, jeans. Someone in the front giggles; faucet runs; door swings; kids chatter; then silence. The sinks clear.

I step out to toss my towel—and slam into a chest.

Not Sawyer.

Tall. Hoodie zipped. Disposable painter's coveralls on top, the cheap kind we hand out for splatter. N95 mask. Ball cap pulled low. Sunglasses even though we're indoors. For a split, stupid second I assume volunteer dad. "Sorry—"

He grips my elbow hard enough to pinch a nerve. Cold shoots up my arm.

"Keep smiling, princess," he says, voice filtered through the mask, pitched low. "Don't make me ruin your pretty wall."

Every cell in my body goes high voltage. "Let go."

He shoves something into my palm—a small rectangle, thick cardstock. Familiar dread spikes. It's the same stock as the envelope at the house. I try to twist free, but he clamps harder. My self-defense training kicks belatedly. I pitch forward like I'm collapsing, free hand snapping up with the wet paper towel I'm still holding, and I mash it into his face, and drive my knee toward his thigh. I miss his groin (damn) but connect with muscle hard enough to jolt him.

He curses, and releases me. I spin, bolting for the door. Behind me his foot slips on wet tile as he ducks out a back

Sawyer

exit. By the time I yank the door open and explode into the hallway, he's gone.

"SAWYER!" My voice cracks. I don't yell like that. I hate yelling like that. But adrenaline is acid, and it's burning fast.

Sawyer appears instantly—how does he do that?—hand already under his shirt where his weapon lives, posture widened. "Cam?"

I thrust the cardstock at him, shaking. "He was in there. Grabbed me. Said—said not to ruin his—no, *my* wall —I—"

"Description," he barks.

I try my best to force air into my lungs and give him every detail I can recall.

Sawyer's eyes go lethal-black. "Riggs, lock perimeter now. Male, six foot give or take, painter whites, N95, cap, sunglasses. Inside rec center bathrooms seconds ago. I'm with principal asset. Repeat: I am with Cam."

"Copy," crackles Riggs. "On the move."

Sawyer slips the card into an evidence sleeve from his pocket (because of course he has one), then sweeps me visually for injuries. "Did he hurt you?"

"Just… uh, my arm." I rotate my elbow, and an ache flares but nothing's broken. "I kneed him. Maybe. He's fast."

He cups my jaw, forcing my eyes to his. "Breathe with me." His voice drops to that steady detonator-timer cadence he used when calming the second-graders. "In, two, three. Out."

It works embarrassingly well. Air trickles back. Color stops snowstorming at the edges of my vision. I lean into his palm because I can't not.

"What'd he say?" Sawyer asks.

"'Keep smiling, princess. Don't make me ruin your pretty wall.'" I swallow. "And he pushed that into my hand."

Sawyer opens the sleeve just enough to read. Block letters, cut-and-glued ransom style like before:

COLOR CAN'T COVER BLOOD. STOP PAINTING TARGETS. WALK AWAY, CAM. NEXT TIME I USE RED.

A smear of something dark streaks the margin—dried paint? Dried *not* paint? My stomach flips.

Sawyer seals it, already cataloging. "Riggs?"

Static, then: "Nothing in hallway cameras. Side exit camera smashed—wire snipped. Got partial witness: food truck guy saw painter coveralls bail westbound between cars, maybe hopped a scooter. Pushing city cams."

Sawyer: "Copy. Call Dean. Code escalate." He angles his

Sawyer

body so I'm behind his larger frame, shielding me from the kids milling at the main doors, blissfully ignorant.

I hate feeling shielded. I also need it right now.

"Sit?" he suggests, steering me toward a bench.

"No. If I sit I'll shake." My laugh is brittle. "I need to finish the interview, right? Social media. Foundation. Show we're not rattled."

"Cam—"

"I mean it." I lift my chin. "He wants me to walk away. I'm not giving him the wall."

We stare each other down. He's measuring the risk, and I'm measuring my backbone. Finally he nods once—sharp, proud, furious. "Then we lock it tighter and finish fast."

"Deal."

He keys his mic. "Riggs, tighten outer ring. We finish in fifteen."

"Roger. And, Cam?" Riggs' voice crackles through. "Whoever that was picked the wrong princess."

Despite everything, I smile. It's shaky, but it's there.

We finish the top coat with parents flanking the kid zone like human bollards while Sawyer and Riggs patrol wider arcs. I give my interview: "Art turns neglected spaces into community. These kids deserve to see their colors towering over traffic." I don't mention masked cowards. I *do* grip Sawyer's wrist off camera when the shakes threaten.

When the last brush is washed and the final group selfie snapped, we pack in a blur. Sawyer herds me to the van like he's escorting state secrets. Inside, I cradle my throbbing elbow and stare out at the mural—our mural—now blazing against twilight.

"You okay?" he asks quietly once the doors close.

"I will be," I say. "You?"

His jaw flexes. "I'm better when I can see the threat."

"Same," I whisper. "Guess we keep painting."

He huffs something that might be a laugh, might be a growl. "Yeah, Cam. We keep painting. And we catch him."

Outside, Riggs double-taps the van panel—clear to roll. As we pull away, I look back at the wall and make myself a promise: whoever thinks color can't stand up to blood is about to learn what happens when you mix the two in equal parts stubborn and steel.

And if I have Sawyer Maddox at my side—no, *if he has me at his*—I like our odds.

7

Sawyer

When we arrive back to her place I keep Cam in my sightline all the way from the curb to the foyer. She walks steady—too steady—the kind of brittle composure you get when shock hasn't decided whether to crash you or crown you. I don't press. Not in front of staff. Not where cameras can memorialize tremors she doesn't want trending.

Edgar meets us at the door with a damp cloth and a look that belongs on a battlefield medic. "Everything all right, Miss Cam?"

"We finished the mural," she says, which is both true and not remotely the point. I give Edgar a tight shake of the head: *no details yet*. He pivots to logistics—tea, ice, dinner—and the routine becomes a ramp we can drive our frayed nerves up without flipping.

While Cam disappears to scrub paint (and evidence powder I dusted along her sleeve) off in the downstairs bath, I step into the side courtyard and dial Dean.

He picks up before the first full ring. "Report."

"Level just moved from nuisance to credible threat with proximity breach," I say. "Contact at rec center women's restroom. Male, approx six foot, athletic build, masked. Grabbed Cam's elbow long enough to pass a written message—same cream cardstock, ransom-block lettering. Line read: *COLOR CAN'T COVER BLOOD. STOP PAINTING TARGETS. NEXT TIME I USE RED.* Tone's controlled. Not junkie erratic."

Dean swears low. "Is she injured?"

"Minor contusion at left cubital. No penetration, no chemical transfer that I could detect visually. She countered with a knee strike, and created separation. Subject exfil'd via side exit with disabled cam. Wire was cleanly cut. He knew the layout."

"So we've got a planner who's watched the site, maybe had access to volunteer logistics." Another pause. "Chain-of-custody on the note?"

"Bagged. I'll courier to lab via **BRAVO** courier at 0600. I also swabbed her sleeve and the cardstock edge; if he had residue—paint, oil, nitrile transfer—we might pull a trace."

"Good." A keyboard clacks. "Riggs staying on your flank?"

Sawyer

"Yeah. I want him embedded here. Also request mobile facial-rec kit for tomorrow's vendor load-ins and a list comparison—anyone with access to Foundation volunteer rosters, Kingsley vendor databases, recent layoffs from Kingsley Aeronautics security. If this is leverage against Gregory through Cam, we tighten both ends."

Dean exhales—approval salted with worry. "Done. How's Cam mentally?"

"Angry, shaken, performing calm." I glance through the French door. She's back in jeans and a soft gray tee, fingers white around a mug. "She's not backing off the mural program."

"Did you expect her to?"

"Nope."

"All right. Call if she spikes or if anything twitches the perimeter. I'm spinning up OSINT to scrape forums for that phrase—*Color can't cover blood.* Might be a signature. Take care of yourself, Sawyer."

"Always."

The line goes dead. I pocket the phone and take one more breath of cooling rosemary hedge before heading inside.

DINNER IS AN AFTERTHOUGHT—HER nibbling, me not. Riggs texts twice with updates (no usable prints on the snipped cam housing; local PD report filed but sanitized per client privacy). Cam jokes with Edgar, asks for extra lemon, thanks him for the grilled halibut she barely touches. Her elbow's swelling. I clock it, but she pretends it's fine.

After plates clear she says, "I'm heading to the studio."

"Want company?"

"You'll hover anyway." She tries for light, and it lands fragile. "Might as well invite the gargoyle."

I follow her across the courtyard flagstones, past lavender pots, through the converted carriage house that serves as her home studio. Inside is riot: canvases leaned in stratified color, drop cloths, dangling clip lights, fans, turpentine, drying racks of palette knives like silver tongues. She flicks on music—volume borderline OSHA violation—some driving drum-and-violin track that drills straight into marrow.

Then she paints.

No warm-up. No sketch. Just a loaded trowel of cadmium red hurled across gesso like arterial spray, followed by punches of indigo, char streaks of carbon black, an almost obscene squeeze of titanium white clawed through with the end of the brush handle. The piece is big—six by eight feet

—and she attacks it like she'd gladly wrestle the threat straight out of existence if the wall would hold still.

I stay in the doorway, hands loose at my sides, letting the blast wash over me.

People assume a bomb guy like me is immune to spectacle. Truth is, we chase clarity. A device is a puzzle—wires, triggers, force vectors. You learn to see patterns at speed, to track trajectories in chaos. Watching Cam paint is like watching a high-speed x-ray of her nervous system externalize. Every strike, every blend reveals load paths—fear, fury, defiance—before she reins them into composition. She's venting pressure and rebalancing simultaneously, a controlled burn. It's... beautiful. Terrifying. Familiar in a way I didn't expect.

The track crests. She stabs, drags, backhands a splash that freckles her cheeks. Sweat beads at her throat. Her braid loosens until her hair sticks to paint down her forearm. She plants one bare foot on the low rung of the easel, leans, and a small sound leaves her—half growl, half sob—so soft the music almost swallows it.

Almost.

My chest tightens.

I don't speak until the song crashes and she slaps the remote, killing the volume. Silence surges in behind the ringing.

She startles when she turns and sees me still there. Color floods her face—genuine blush, not acrylic. "How long—?"

"Long enough to know the wall lost," I say.

A laugh slips out of her, wet with leftover adrenaline. She drags the back of her wrist over her forehead, leaving a comet of white. "You ever watch somebody cry and punch a pillow at the same time? That's what that was."

"Healthier than bottling." I cross in, slow, letting her choose whether to step back. She doesn't. "Arm."

"It's fine."

"You're an unreliable narrator." I angle her left elbow toward the light. The bruise is blooming violet beneath the skin, outlined where the assailant's fingers clamped. Anger flares so hot my molars pulse. I rein it in and reach for the compact trauma kit clipped to my belt. Cold gel pack, wrap, small packet of topical arnica I carry because I've done this gig long enough to know clients bruise.

"You come standard with that?" she teases as I crack the pack and knead it alive.

"Upcharge for glitter bandages," I deadpan.

She grins, then sucks a breath when the cold hits. "Ohhh-hhh, that hurts good."

"Keep it there for at least ten minutes." I hold the pack in place while she leans against a high table spattered with ten thousand past colors. Up close I can count gold flecks in her irises. She smells like citrus hand soap fought with mineral spirits and lost. My thumb brushes an errant streak of red at her triceps, and I force it to stop before it wanders farther.

"Tell me something," she says after a beat, voice gone low, almost intimate. "Why EOD?"

No one starts with the easy ones. "Because I hated bullies," I say, surprising myself with the brevity. "And I hate unfair fights. Bombs are the ultimate unfair fight—cowards wiring shrapnel to timers, giving you no face to punch back. EOD lets you reach in and take that away from them." I study the bruise again. "Makes it a fair fight."

She swallows, eyes never leaving mine. "Was it scary?"

"Every time," I admit. "You get good at compartmentalizing. Breathe, process, follow protocol. Most days the scary part comes after, when you replay what you almost triggered. You learn to respect fear without letting it drive." I nod at her canvas. "You just did the same thing. Took the hit, processed, redirected."

"Yeah?" She looks over her shoulder at the work-in-progress. "Feels more like tantrum art."

"Tantrums don't land that compositionally balanced." I point. "You triangulated load—red anchored high left, black low right, white drawing the eye through. That's structural."

She smirks. "Spoken like a man who thinks in blast cones."

"Guilty." I lower the pack. "Where'd *your* art come from?"

She inhales, exhales slowly, as if sifting through boxes. "My mom painted. Not professionally. She'd spread butcher paper on the kitchen floor and give me condiments—ketchup, mustard, food coloring—and let me 'paint dinner.' Dad would come home, step in purple mustard, lose his mind, then laugh because she'd already photographed the mess for some charity newsletter. When she died, the kitchen got remodeled—stainless, sterile, boardroom chic. Colors disappeared." Her mouth pulls to one side. "So I chased them. Chalk on sidewalks. Spray paint on plywood behind the garage. Oils when I could steal them. Every time Dad took me to a shareholders' meeting I'd come home and blast another wall in color just to prove the house still breathed."

I let that sit. "How old?"

"Fourteen." She shrugs. "Rebellion stuck. But it turned into something bigger when I saw how kids' faces change when they put color somewhere no one told them they were allowed to. It's like oxygen. That's what I want—oxygen in dead spaces."

I look at the bruise again. *Color can't cover blood.* Our perp wants to suffocate oxygen out of her world. That's his power play.

"He picked the wrong hallway," I say.

"Damn right he did."

We stand close enough that her breath ghosts my throat. Her free hand lifts, and she lightly taps my sternum with a paint-wet fingertip, leaving a scarlet dot over my heart. "Target acquired," she murmurs.

"Cam…" Warning. Plea. Promise. All tangled.

She searches my face. "If I cross a line, you'll stop me?"

"I'll try." It comes out ragged.

Her smile tilts sly. "Try hard?"

"Hard is the problem."

We hover in that charged pocket—gravity tugging, protocols bracing—until my phone vibrates sharp against my hip. I step back like I've been doused.

"Yeah." I thumb accept the call. "Riggs?"

"Pulled municipal traffic cam two blocks west of the rec center," he says. "Got a maybe-match—painter whites, mask off once he cleared the crowd, hopped an electric scooter. Frame grab inbound. Sending to Dean and you. Plate on the scooter's rental code traces to a dummy account. Dean wants to run face through our database. Check your secure inbox."

"Copy." I glance at Cam, and she's wiping the red dot off my chest with the edge of a clean rag, expression half apology, half dare. "Keep digging. I'll review."

The call ends. The moment, however, doesn't.

"Business?" she asks.

"Lead." I set the gel pack on the table. "We may get an ID."

"Good." She leans the bruised arm against her ribs protectively. "If you catch him, I want to see him."

"We'll see." Which means *if chain-of-evidence allows and you seeing him won't land us in litigation.* What I really want is to put my fist through his teeth. Not professional. Very true.

She turns back to the canvas, dips a brush in white, then holds it up. "You adding a stroke or you just critiquing?"

"This wall big enough for boundaries?"

"I'll give you a corner." She laughs softly. "Draw me a… perimeter."

Of course she would. I take the offered brush, step in, and with two controlled pulls lay a thin, continuous arc of white that curves behind the chaos of red—subtle, almost hidden—tying disparate blasts together into a hooked shield. Not a cage. A contour. Protection disguised as motion.

She studies it, head tipped. "Always drawing lines."

"Lines keep you safe."

"Sometimes crossing them makes the art." She glances sideways, lashes low. "Sometimes both."

We're close again. Close enough that if I angled an inch our mouths would—

My radio chirps: *Perimeter green.* Riggs, again, saving the day.

I exhale. "Ice. Ten more." I nod at her elbow.

"Bossy."

"Alive."

She salutes sloppily with paint-slick fingers. "Yes, sir."

I should leave, but I don't. I take a stool, sit where I can see the door and the window and the artist who's become my axis, and watch her layer color over the arc I drew—but not cover it. Never cover. She lets it ghost through, a line only visible if you know to look.

Hours from now I'll replay this night and wonder if this was the exact moment I stopped being a contractor on a high-net-worth detail and became something else. Bodyguard, sure. Shield, absolutely. But also… collaborator.

And no, Dean, I'm not requesting reassignment.

Not when the most dangerous thing I've ever stood in front of is asking me, in paint and half-smiles, to stay.

8

Camille

The first omen of chaos arrives cloaked in rose-gold sunglasses and a grin built for trouble. Vanessa Mercado—public-relations maven, sometimes partner in crime—sashays through my front gates as if they'd opened just for her. To be fair, they probably did. Edgar has a soft spot for anyone who compliments his topiary dragons.

I'm on the veranda, laptop balanced on my knees while I proof donor lists for the gala, when her heels click across the flagstones. "Cam! Permission to raid your wine fridge?"

"Granted—if you promise not to reorganize my cheeses by zodiac sign again." I close the laptop, stand, and brace for the hug that always feels like being tackled by scented glitter.

She squeezes, pulls back, studies my face. "You look… wired."

"Long week." I wave it off, not wanting to revisit masked psychos and bruised elbows. "Mural turned out amazing, though."

"I saw the livestream! Those kids were adorable." She wiggles her eyebrows. "Almost as adorable as the living, breathing action figure hovering behind you."

Before I can whirl, Sawyer steps out of the house, talking quietly into his comms mic. Tactical jeans, fitted black tee, holster riding his hip like it was born there. He spots Vanessa, nods politely, returns to conversation with Riggs —who appears farther down the path hauling a box of infrared cameras. They're doing a full perimeter upgrade tonight. Sawyer said he didn't care how many zeros the invoice accrued. Oxygen, he called it, and for once he wasn't talking about paint.

Vanessa watches him stalk toward a lamppost anchor point, jaw hinged open. "*Dios mío*, who ordered the dark-and-deadly bodyguard?"

"My father," I mutter. "Please behave."

But Vanessa is already gliding forward, hair swishing like a Pantene commercial. She taps Sawyer's elbow. "Hi, I'm Vanessa, security consultant connoisseur. And you are?"

He finishes whatever code phrase he was murmuring—"…Delta clear, post Four"—then turns, professional smile in place. "Sawyer Maddox, ma'am."

"Ma'am?" She fans herself theatrically. "Do I look like a ma'am?"

His eyebrow quirks exactly one millimeter, and I feel it vibrate in my sternum. "Protocol, Vanessa."

"Oh, he knows my name." She winks at me over her shoulder. *Kill me now.*

I stride over, slip an arm through Vanessa's. "Let me show you the new garden lights before you start interrogating my employee."

"Employee?" She snickers. "Sweetheart, if he were *my* employee I'd never get any work done."

Sawyer clears his throat. "Riggs is at the south hedge, Cam. We'll finish installing the west-gate camera, then circle back. Radios on channel three." He barely glances at Vanessa, but she flushes like he declared his undying love.

We peel off toward the gazebo. Vanessa digs an elbow into my ribs. "I approve of the new décor—tall, broad, and intense. Does he come with a dimmer switch?"

"Vanessa."

"What? A girl's gotta ask." We reach the koi pond where lily pads bob under fairy lights. She stops, turns serious. "Okay, flirtation aside, how are you really? News says you doubled security on the mural site. Something happen?"

I hesitate, and run my fingers over the tender bruise on my elbow. "Someone tried to scare me."

Her eyes sharpen. "Cam…"

"I'm fine. Honestly." I force a smile. "Sawyer's taking it very seriously. Probably too seriously."

"Too seriously is his job." She studies me. "And judging by the way you're watching him work, you don't hate the view."

Heat creeps up my neck. "He's… professional."

"Oh, honey, that man's jawline is a war crime. And you keep licking your lips every time he bends to adjust a cable."

"I do not!" The koi startle at my squeak.

Before Vanessa can roast me further, Riggs ambles over, beard bristling with zip-tie ends. "Ladies. Cabling's done. Perimeter's now a paparazzi-proof laser grid."

Vanessa spins, zeroes in. "And who's this? Lumberjack chic. I like."

"Andrew Riggs, but everyone calls me Riggs," he says, offering a calloused paw. "I operate power tools and occasionally diplomacy."

"Vanessa Mercado. I operate social media and occasionally hearts." She gives him a once-over so blatant I expect sparks. "Need a drink? Cam said I could raid the wine."

Sawyer

"Wine's above my pay grade on duty," Riggs replies, but his grin says *ask me again when the cameras stop rolling.*

I groan. "Can we at least finish fortifying the fortress before you start speed-dating the security team?"

"Nobody said I can't multitask." Vanessa blows me a kiss and glides inside, Riggs in tow, launching into a tale about how she once turned a charity auction into a conga line. The man chuckles—deep and genuine. Traitor.

I turn, and collide with Sawyer's chest. Somehow he's materialized behind me without a sound. Almost ghostlike. His gaze tracks Vanessa and Riggs disappearing into the house. "Your friend is… energetic."

"She collects phone numbers like charity tax receipts," I mutter. "Sorry."

"No apology needed." But something flickers in his eyes—amusement, maybe. Or something tighter. He angles his body closer, subvocalizes into his mic: "Riggs, status?"

Riggs: "Client's friend insists the wine cellar is haunted. We're investigating."

Sawyer's mouth twitches. "Copy. Avoid spirits other than ghosts."

"Funny guy," I say. "Didn't peg you for one."

"Few do." He steps back, and seems to remember himself. Professional. Always. But his gaze lingers a beat too long on my mouth, and the hummingbird under my ribs resumes kamikaze missions.

"Oh, Cam—one sec." Vanessa bursts out of the French doors again, a bottle of rosé in each hand. "Do you have a corkscrew in the studio? The fancy one shaped like a man flexing?"

"I'll grab it," I sigh. Anything to remove myself before my face combusts. "Be right back."

Sawyer: "I'll escort."

"I'm going thirty feet."

"Thirty feet too many." His tone leaves no room for an argument. I roll my eyes but head to the studio, him shadowing like a silent thundercloud.

Inside, I rummage through drawers, and finally find the novelty opener. When I turn, Sawyer stands by the unfinished painting from last night, studying the new strokes I added after his line—turquoise streaming from the arc like neon smoke.

"You expanded it."

"Felt right." I set the corkscrew down, and cross my arms, suddenly self-conscious. "You don't mind?"

He inches closer to the canvas, fingertip hovering near a section where I blended cobalt into crimson. "Looks like movement through danger. Very controlled."

"I was thinking of river water carving rock. Same path, a new depth," I say, surprised by how much I want him to understand.

"I get that." His voice is low, almost reverent. "Erosion and endurance."

We're standing too close. I can smell cedar and a hint of gun oil. I see the faint shadow of his stubble that's darker than yesterday. Awareness buzzes between us like a live beast unable to be tamed.

"Thank you," I whisper.

"For what?"

"For caring whether I wake up tomorrow."

He exhales as if punched. "That's the job."

"No." I tap the arc he drew, white and clean. "This isn't the job. This is you."

He looks at me then—truly looks—and the room narrows to the space between our knees. His hand lifts, hesitates, then cups my elbow where the bruise blooms. His thumb passes over the healing skin so gently my breath stutters.

"I hate that he touched you," he says.

"Me too." I swallow. My pulse is a canon. "But you're here now."

"Always." The single word thrums with a reverent vow.

A crash reverberates from the house—a bottle hitting tile, maybe, followed by Vanessa's shriek of laughter and Riggs' baritone: "I told you the cork was possessed!"

The spell cracks, and we step apart. Sawyer jerks his chin toward the noise. "You safe here for five?"

"I'll live."

He jogs off to ensure my wine cellar is still standing. I drag a shaky breath, fan my face, then follow with more decorum than my legs feel.

BY THE TIME I reach the massive open-plan kitchen, Vanessa is sitting on the quartz island, dangling her legs while Riggs mops up a puddle of rosé. "I swear it popped itself," she declares, cheeks flushed with color.

Sawyer stands at the doorway, arms folded, assessing. Seeing me, he relaxes half a notch. "Faulty bottle," he explains.

"More like an overzealous corkscrew," Riggs drawls, nudging Vanessa's thigh with his elbow. "Told her to let me handle it."

Vanessa pats his bicep. "Where's the fun in that?"

Jealousy nips my ribs. It's irrational—Sawyer's not flirting—but Vanessa's earlier laser focus makes me irrationally

Sawyer

territorial. Before I can scold myself, headlights bloom across the drive, cutting through the front windows in a sweep. Too quick for Edgar's usual florist delivery, too slow for a visitor.

Sawyer's posture changes—steel straight, hand dropping to his concealed weapon. "Riggs."

Riggs cocks his head, listening. "Not on the schedule."

I step toward the foyer arch, but Sawyer blocks me with one arm. "Stay here."

Vanessa pauses mid-sip. "What's wrong?"

"Probably nothing," I lie for her. But icy dread crawls my spine.

Riggs slings the mop, strides to the hall console where his rifle case leans, and unlatches it fluidly. Sawyer pulls a tablet from his belt, and taps through the security cam feeds. The closest feed freezes with pixelated static.

"Cam six offline," he mutters. "Four and five still live." He flicks to another view.

I inhale sharply. "Cut lines?"

"Looks that way." Sawyer's voice is low, controlled, the same tone he probably used while diffusing bombs. "Riggs, you cover north window lines. I'll check cartons."

"I have pepper spray," Vanessa offers weakly.

Sawyer spares her half a glance. "Stay behind the island."

Riggs tosses her an actual canister from his belt. "Pull pin, press nozzle. Don't spray us."

Edgar appears, eyes wide. "Mr. Maddox—is everything okay?"

"No," Sawyer and I answer simultaneously.

A muffled thump hits the veranda—heavy footfall. Another. My heart sprints into my throat.

Sawyer presses a finger to his lips, and motions me backward until my spine kisses the refrigerator. His palm lingers at my hip, anchoring me there. Heat floods, absurdly out of place with danger spiking, but that's adrenaline for you.

Riggs kills the kitchen lights, and moonlight pools through the skylights. The house holds its breath. Another thump. A scrape of metal at the lock.

"Edgar, security code red," Sawyer whispers. Edgar darts to a hidden panel, keys a sequence. Somewhere, shutters thunk closed.

I can't stand behind refrigerators when burly strangers invade my home. I grab a cast-iron skillet—thank you, Le Creuset—and grip the handle. Sawyer sees, and tightens his jaw but doesn't argue.

He whispers, *"Stay behind my right."*

Sawyer

The front door bangs open, wood splintering. A figure bursts inside wearing dark clothes, a ski mask, and something metallic in his hand. The timing is too perfect. They braved cameras, locks—this is choreographed aggression.

Sawyer steps into the foyer with the fluidity of water turning to blade. "Drop it," he barks, weapon trained.

The intruder hesitates. Wrong move. Riggs flanks left through the parlor arch, his rifle leveled. The man spins, sees two, and stumbles.

Sawyer advances, pivoting to keep his body between me and the threat. "On the ground, hands wide."

Instead the man lobs the metal object—something small, round—toward the hall. Flash-bang. I recognize it too late. Light swallows sound, or maybe it's the other way around. My vision flares white, and every nerve screams static.

Sawyer's body crashes into mine, driving us down behind the island just as the device detonates—*bang!*—deafening. His arms wrap around my skull, tucking it into his chest. The scent of gunpowder and cedar slams home.

For endless seconds I hear nothing but my heartbeat. I see nothing but afterimages. Sawyer's weight blankets me. It's solid and reassuring. Slowly sounds edgeback—a ringing, then Riggs shouting, "Moving!"

Sawyer lifts just enough to look down at me, hands framing my face. "You okay?"

"I—I think so." Everything wobbles, but no pain. Ears hiss. My fingers clutch his shirt, refusing to let go.

He stands, pulling me with him, and positions me in the corner behind the island. "Stay."

I do. Because his tone leaves no room, and because my knees are tapioca. From my vantage I watch him and Riggs sweep forward—a coordinated ballet of lethal efficiency. They clear the foyer, and find the flash-bang still fizzing. There's no intruder. The hall camera feed flickers then steadies, and shows a figure sprinting back through the open gates onto the street. Sirens wail in the distance. Edgar must have tripped the silent alarm.

Minutes stretch. Sawyer finally holsters his weapon, returning to me, hands running over my arms for injuries. His pupils are blown wide as his chest heaves. The energy rolling off him is molten.

"I'm fine," I rasp, then curse the tremor in my voice. "Really."

He cups the back of my head, foreheads touching, our breath mingling. "He breached the yard." Fury vibrates through every word. "I will not let that happen again."

The intimacy of the moment—his body still half-caging mine, Vanessa and Edgar whispering somewhere in the dark—should feel absurd. Instead it feels inevitable, like a note finally resolving after bars of tension. My palms slide up his ribcage, feeling the unyielding muscle beneath.

"Thank you," I whisper. "For being the wall."

His thumb brushes my cheekbone, softer than a sigh. "You make it worth guarding."

Lightning forks through me—need, fear, gratitude, lust inextricably woven. I sway closer, nearly brush his lips, when Vanessa's voice slices through. "Um, guys? Police are at the gate."

Sawyer steps back, his mask of professionalism slamming down. He turns to Riggs, issues crisp directives. The lights snap back on, and the moment is lost.

Later there will be statements, sensor audits, sleepless hours. But right now his hand finds the small of my back, guiding me gently toward the study where we'll wait for the detectives. The touch says *mine to protect*, and my body answers so loudly it nearly drowns out the sirens.

I am in so much trouble, and not just from masked intruders.

Because somewhere between flash-bang and pulse-pound, I stopped seeing Sawyer Maddox as an impenetrable wall.

And started seeing him as the door I want to walk through—even if it's marked *danger: keep out*.

9

Sawyer

I've stood inside smoking blast craters that felt calmer than Camille's foyer does right now.

Flashes pop as crime-scene techs photograph the splintered doorframe. Officers in Kevlar mill around, radios crackling, while Detective Hartley interviews Cam for the second time this week. My pulse thrums an ugly counter-rhythm. Anger. Shame. Even sharper anger. I was forty feet away when the lock blew. Forty. In my world, that's daylight-bright failure.

Riggs watches my face from beside the entry console where he's dusting the flash-bang shell for prints. He nods once —*steady, brother*—but doesn't approach. He knows a live mine when he sees one.

"Mr. Maddox?" A uniformed officer snaps me back. "Your statement?"

Sawyer

"Already gave it," I clip, then force a calmer addendum. "Happy to clarify timelines once your CSU's finished."

He mutters into a notepad, and wanders off. Too many bodies, too many questions, not enough answers. I scan the perimeter cam feed on my tablet—rewatching the breach frame by frame. Masked perp scales the gate's side wall, thumps over the top, lands like he rehearsed the drop. He sprints across the courtyard, disables the camera with a handheld jammer—not a kid's toy; high-frequency gear. Then he produces a slim jim, bypasses the deadbolt. Twenty seconds to entry. These aren't scared stalkers. They're tactical.

My chest tightens.

I need air. I need Dean.

I slip through the library's French doors into the courtyard. Night wind bites my sweat-damp shirt. I dial.

Dean answers. "Talk."

"Perimeter breach at twenty-two forty. One intruder, male six-one, athletic. Deployed flash-bang, no lethal weapon brandished. Escaped on foot before patrol arrived. Damage to doorframe and foyer, no injuries." My voice stays even but my hands tremble despite clenching them. "We had full camera grid plus ground sensors. He bypassed two feeds with a jammer, snipped one physical line. He knew the layout."

Dean whistles low. "Ballsy. What's the message?"

"Unclear. Could be pure intimidation. Could be recon like testing the response time."

"How fast were local PD wheels?"

"Six minutes from silent alarm. He was gone in two. Left the shell, nothing else. We've got partial shoeprint and maybe fiber transfer from the jamming pouch." I exhale. The night smells of rosemary and burnt magnesium. "I should have been there, Dean."

"You can't occupy every vector at once. You neutralized the threat, protected the principal."

"Door's still busted. That's a fail."

"Then tighten it. But don't let guilt cloud your pattern analysis. Whoever this is escalated *inside* your comfort zone. That means they're not deterred by the optics of security."

I rake a hand through my hair. "The gala's in six days. Hundreds of people, open house, press. Should we pull the plug?"

"Convince your client. Cam's call, not yours."

"If she insists, I need four more operators and a mobile command rig."

"Granted. I'll put Bravo Orange team on standby."

"Copy."

"Sawyer," Dean adds, voice softening, "I can rotate you off-site if you think emotions are muddying your judgment."

"No." The answer fires out. "I'm committed."

Silence. He knows what *committed* means in my vocabulary. Locked. Lethal. All-in. "Then get some sleep, recharge the sensors, and write me a new op plan before oh-eight. We'll dissect it on a call."

"Roger that."

We disconnect. I spend two heroic breaths pretending the stars aren't spinning, then pocket the phone and head back inside.

THE HOUSE EMPTIES SLOWLY. CSU packs their kits, patrol cars reverse down the drive, and Hartley promises updates. Riggs escorts Vanessa to her rideshare (she winks at him but spares me a thumbs-up —*your hero's safe*). Edgar re-keys the alarm while muttering about reinforced steel doors and maybe a moat.

It's after one a.m. when the mansion finally exhales into a hush. I dispatch Riggs to bunk in the guesthouse monitoring screens. Then I hunt for Cam, stepping room to room until I find light spilling under the study door.

She sits in an armchair by the cold fireplace, knees drawn up, a half-full glass of cabernet pinched between both hands like a tiny life raft. She's changed into an oversized sweatshirt that hits mid-thigh; bare legs tuck underneath her. Her eyes, normally kaleidoscope bright, look stormy.

She doesn't startle when I walk in. Just watches me quietly.

I close the door, cross the Persian rug, and kneel beside the chair. "You should be sleeping."

"So should you," she murmurs. The wine sloshes as her knuckles tense. "Did you call Dean?"

"Yeah." I rest my forearms on my knees. "He'll boost manpower. Orange team's solid."

"Orange team?" A faint smile ghosts. "Mango Avengers?"

"The Vitamin C squad." My attempt at humor lands about as well as the flash-bang. "Cam, about the gala—"

"I know," she cuts in, tension sharpening her tone. "You want it canceled."

"I *need* it canceled. We host six hundred high-net-worth guests, plus press, plus staff, on a property already compromised? That's a jackpot for whoever's orchestrating these hits."

Her laugh cracks, raw. "You think I don't know that? The gala funds the Kingsley Community Arts Network—the program that put paint brushes in those kids' hands yesterday. Canceling means losing two million in pledged donations."

"Money can be rescheduled. You can't."

She flinches, but recovers. "We've spent months planning. Media campaigns, vendor contracts, caterers. People booked flights. Dad's using the event to soften investor sentiment before the IPO roadshow."

I ground my jaw so hard it clicks. "Your father would rather risk your safety than reschedule a party?"

"That's not fair. He doesn't understand how bad it's gotten. And the gala isn't just for him." She sets her wine on a side table, and wraps her arms around her shins. "It's my mother's legacy. The first fundraiser she founded was right here in this house. Every year I set the stage—paint the backdrops, design the invitations, curate student art for auction. If I cancel because I'm scared, then whoever's doing this wins."

She looks away, blinking. A tear falls, and she swipes it angrily, smearing her mascara.

Something inside me fractures. I rise, fetch a box of tissues, and kneel again. Her arms untuck enough for me to dab gently beneath her eye. She breathes shakily but doesn't pull away.

"You're not weak if you pivot," I say. "You're strategic. We can move the gala to a hotel with built-in security layers."

She shakes her head. "I can't look every donor in the eye and say the Kingsleys are afraid. We stand or it crumbles."

Stubborn, brave, reckless. It's infuriating—and magnificent.

I exhale, slow. "Then we harden the target." She meets my gaze, hope flickering. "Four new operators, K-9 sweeps, credential scanners at each gate, ballistic window film, drone overwatch."

"And the staff?"

"I'll vet every vendor. If they breathe wrong, they don't get in."

"And me?" She tries for a joke but her voice shakes. "You'll make me wear armor under my gown?"

"Kevlar corset." My grin is weak. "Bulletproof chic."

Her laughter bubbles out—real this time, easing the knot in my chest. I brush a stray wave behind her ear, fingertips trailing her jawline. The contact sparks—an entire circuit roaring to life. She stills, eyes widening as if she feels it too.

"There's something else," I admit, voice dropping. "Tonight proved I can't be everywhere at once. The second I left your side—"

"It's not your fault."

"I promised you safety." I lean in, forehead almost touching hers. "I'm going to keep it."

Her breath hitches. "How, Sawyer?"

"By not letting you out of my sight." The vow tastes dangerous, almost intimate. "From now until the gala's over, you and I move as one unit."

"Bathroom?" she teases, the faintest quiver returning.

"Door stays propped." It's half joke, half absolute seriousness.

Color warms her cheeks. "What about when I sleep?"

"I'll be in the hall, inches away. Or—" Words choke as a new possibility flares. "Or closer, if you want."

Her lashes flicker. Silence stretches, pulsing, until she lifts her hand—hesitant—and touches my chest where her paint mark once clung. Through cotton, heat sears my skin.

"I feel safer when you're near," she whispers.

I inhale—sharp, ragged. My hand covers hers, and holds it firmly. "Then near is where I'll be."

She shifts, legs unfolding, feet brushing the rug. We hover, breath mingling. If she tilts forward a hair more, we'll cross a line I swore not to breach while the threat remains unchecked. Yet every instinct screams to close the distance, to claim her mouth, to anchor her shaking in something solid—*me*.

"Cam…" Warning and plea thread together.

She swallows, pupils blown. "Yes?"

I force air out. "I need you to sign off on increased protocols. We'll install metal detectors at both entrances, coordinate with SPPD, run background checks on catering crew."

"Okay." Her voice barely carries. "Anything else?"

"Yeah." My thumb strokes the side of her hand. "This." Reluctantly, I let go, step back. The space between us chills. "Can't happen yet."

She nods—understanding flickering with disappointment. "Threat level."

"Until you're clear, I'm steel. After…" I meet her gaze, let her read the fire banked behind discipline. "We'll repaint the house in red if you want."

She flushes, smiling small but real. "I'll hold you to that."

"Deal." I pick up her forgotten wine glass, set it aside, then hold out my hand. "Bedtime. Sunrise in five hours and I need you lucid."

"You won't sleep either."

"I'll doze on guard. Comes with the job." I pull her gently to her feet. She sways, and I steady her. "Lean on me if you need."

Instead she links her fingers with mine. "Walk me?"

"Always."

Sawyer

We traverse dim corridors lit by sconces; my hand engulfs hers. At her bedroom door she pauses, studying the new steel reinforcement plate Riggs bolted over the frame.

"Stronger," she whispers.

"Unbreakable," I correct, brushing my knuckles along the wood. "Go shower, get warm, and sleep."

She pushes to her toes—impulsive—plants a soft kiss to my cheek. Lightning ripples across every nerve. "Goodnight, Soldier Boy."

I step back, throat tight. "Goodnight, Cam."

The door closes. I exhale the breath I've been kayfabe holding all night, then take position outside her room, back to the wall, eyes on the hall intersection. Every shadow feels personal now. I rest my palm on the grip of my SIG, feeling the comforting certainty of metal.

She thinks I'm the wall. Truth is, she's become mine.

And walls don't fall. Not while I'm breathing.

10

Camille

Sunlight drapes the veranda in honey, but I'm already on my third espresso and fifth checklist before the first ray crosses the marble threshold. Six days—now five—until two hundred philanthropists and four hundred socialites descend on Kingsley House for the annual gala. Normally I'd be thrilled; this year the event feels like a live-wire negotiation between purpose and peril.

I pad barefoot through the ballroom, clipboard tucked under one arm, earbuds feeding me a rapid-fire update from my assistant, Megan, who's wrangling vendors off-site. While Megan rattles off linen delays and canapé counts, the far doors open and Sawyer strides in with the BRAVO Orange Team—four operators in muted polos that somehow still scream cavalry.

Sawyer wears charcoal tactical pants and a long-sleeve black henley that hugs his biceps with indecent devotion.

Sawyer

He moves with quiet authority, pointing out blind spots, issuing radio checks, marking doorways with discreet adhesive sensors. The Orange operators fall into formation around him like planets around a sun. For a second I just … watch.

His focus is laser, but when he catches me staring, his expression softens, a flicker of warmth beneath the ice. My pulse speeds up. I force myself back to the task list, but every tick of the pen echoes *want, want, want.*

The day blurs into stations:

Florist consult. ("No peonies near the heat sensors, Ms. Kingsley.")

AV team test. ("Screens must not block camera sightlines.")

Catering walkthrough. ("Badge every sous chef.")

Everywhere I go, Sawyer or an Orange operator floats at the edge of my vision—unobtrusive but monumental, like living statues ready to leap the moment reality tilts. It should feel oppressive. Instead it steadies me. And stokes something wicked.

Because how do you stay purely professional when the person guarding your heartbeat looks at you as if it's already his territory?

LATER IN THE EVENING, the last vendor van rolls away. The estate exhales into a hush of cicadas and shifting light. I find Sawyer in the back garden, calibrating a discreet drone pad beneath the wisteria arbor. He checks something on his tablet, completely absorbed.

I lean against a column, arms folded. "You're supposed to take breaks, Soldier Boy."

He answers without looking up. "Break comes when you can sip wine without looking over your shoulder."

I push off the column, crossing to him, my voice soft. "What if I look over my shoulder … and find you?"

That arrests him. His head lifts, and his gray-green eyes lock onto mine. Heat sizzles down my spine. For a long beat neither of us moves—then a chime sounds on his tablet. He swipes, expression shuttering. "Motion sensor test complete." But his voice is gravelled, affected.

"Come inside when you're done," I say, hoping the invitation buries itself under the innocent wording. "Dinner's at eight."

DINNER, while lovely, is a memory I barely tasted. Vanessa's texted that she's safely tucked in at her condo; Riggs is on the night perimeter shift. Edgar retired early. The mansion feels too big, too dark, too echoing with what-ifs. I pace my bedroom suite, replaying every awful scenario this coming week could birth.

A faint knock raps. Sawyer steps in, gaze sweeping, confirming all clear before focusing on me in my oversized Stanford sweatshirt and boxer-short pajama bottoms.

"Hall post secured," he says. "You should sleep."

"You too." I pat the edge of the bed. "Which is why you should sit in here instead of the hallway. That chair—" I point to a high-backed armchair near the window—"looks marginally more comfortable than a floorboard."

His jaw ticks. "Cam…"

"Platonic proximity," I assure. "Guardian-angel chic."

He hesitates … then nods. "Ten minutes. Then I'll rotate with Riggs."

He crosses, drags the chair closer to the foot of the bed, and sits. Shadow pools around his shoulders, the moonlight cutting along his cheekbones. The silhouette alone is a whole romance novel.

I slip under the duvet, but sleep is a mirage. I can feel him watching—alert, heart beating in sync with the pulse thrumming in my ears. The room smells faintly of cedar and linen. That combination is becoming a Pavlovian arousal.

Minutes tick by. We say nothing, yet every second furls the tether tighter. Finally I can't stand the distance. I can't breathe.

"Would it ruin your professional reputation," I whisper, "to lie beside me—just to help me sleep?"

Silence spikes. He shifts, tension coiling. "You know the line we're dancing."

"I know you drew it," I counter. My voice shakes but I keep going. "It'll be there in the morning. Tonight, I need to borrow warmth."

His exhale is a ragged cliff edge. He rises—slow, deliberate—and approaches the bedside. "On top of the covers," he says, as if reminding himself. "Armed."

"Promise not to steal your sidearm." My smile is shaky, but real.

He slides in, fully clothed, lying stiff as a board. I turn on my side, facing him. The duvet separates us, yet heat radiates between our bodies like an illicit current. I take one brave inch closer.

"You okay?" he murmurs.

"Not even a little," I admit. "Someone wants to ruin everything good and colorful. But right now, with you here, I can almost pretend they won't."

He lifts his hand, hovers, then cups the nape of my neck, thumb stroking tiny circles. Fireworks ignite low in my belly.

"It *won't* end like that," he vows, voice earthquake steady. "I'm walls and doors, remember?"

"More than that," I whisper. "You're the reason I keep breathing deep."

A soft, incredulous sound escapes him. He leans in, forehead resting against mine. We breathe each other's air. If I angle my mouth two centimeters, I'll taste him. Every cell begs.

He whispers, "After the gala."

I nod, but my control snaps. I press the gentlest kiss against the corner of his mouth—barely a brush, a promise etched in air. He trembles, and I feel it. But he turns his head, captures my lips fully with his for a heartbeat—hot, sure, infinite—before pulling back. He never deepened the kiss, yet somehow, it was the hottest kiss I'd ever experienced.

His eyes are molten. "Sleep now, Cam."

Somehow, wrapped in electric silence, I do. His heartbeat thunders under my ear, and the last thing my mind records is the safe weight of his arm above the covers, curved protectively around my hip without truly holding, yet holding everything that matters.

11

Sawyer

05:14 — Dawn drags pewter light across the eastern ridge and finds me on the roof, wind stinging my face while Orange-Team's newest drone completes its final diagnostics. A month ago I would have relished the quiet click-hum of rotors waking up over a city that still half-sleeps. Today I'm wrestling an entirely different engine —the one idling under my ribs since Cam's mouth brushed mine last night.

I told her *after the gala*.

I meant it.

But the taste of her—sweet wine and reckless hope—keeps replaying like shrapnel lodged in the memory, impossible to ignore.

"Telemetry clean," Rae reports through the earpiece. She's Orange-Team's UAS wizard—pink pixie-cut blowing in the breeze as she checks her tablet. "We've got a four-hour dwell, switchable IR cam, and a perimeter loop every ninety seconds."

"Good." I sign off on her digital checklist, then scan the estate below. In four nights, this place will glow like Versailles—and feel twice as porous.

Across the lawn, two more Orange operators, Malik and Anderssen, install portable stanchions that will form the guest magnetometer lanes. I key my mic. "Malik, status?"

"Conduit run set; fiber patched to Command. ETA on fencing install is fifteen."

"Copy. Anderssen?"

"Access-control kiosk online, facial-rec pre-calibrated."

"Good. I want secondary credential scan ready by eighteen-hundred. No barcodes, no entry."

They echo acknowledgements—steady cadence of competence—but my focus drifts inevitably back to the west wing windows. One of those panes hides Cam's studio; sunlight now spears through the skylight into that riot of color where she'll be awake soon, brushing pigment into rebellion.

I swallow the urge to climb down this roof and barge in, just to see her hair haloed in gold for two measly seconds. Iron discipline—that thing that kept me alive in IED alley—presses steel over my pulse. She's still in danger. *Eyes up.*

08:32 — Gallery hall. The catering director, a clipped Brit named Hannah, quizzes me about load-in lanes for gala day.

"You'll process the waitstaff through Gate Two," I say, pointing to the floor plan. "Orange-Two escorts them to the service corridor. Lockers are here. No personal phones allowed past that checkpoint."

Hannah frowns. "They rely on phones for plating instructions."

"They'll get printed packets." I don't budge. "Any staff caught with unvetted electronics crosses this red line and they're off the property, no debate."

She sighs but accepts. Anderssen signs off her updated map. Moving parts nested within moving parts—exactly how you diffuse a bomb: define each wire, isolate current, never let circuits cross in unintended ways.

Except last night I let circuits cross—my mouth on hers, pulse synced, promise slipping. It felt less like detonation and more like finally stepping into the proper alignment.

"Sawyer!" Malik calls from the doorway. "AV crew's here early. Want eyes?"

"On it." I pivot down the hall.

13:05 — Command trailer. Riggs props his boots on a case of wired-fiber while scrubbing lunch crumbs from his beard. "You're running hot," he observes. "What's the play after the gala? What if the gala isn't their target? What if they decide to hit after?"

I arch a brow. "Then we'll have contingency plans."

He smirks. "And when do you plan on sweeping the lady off her paint-splattered feet?" The glint in his eye makes me roll a shoulder—half shrug, half threat. He chuckles. "Easy, brother. Just don't let the fox see you guarding the henhouse with your zipper undone."

"Zipper's up. I'm focused on the task." But even as I bark it, my brain replays Cam's sleepy whisper: *Borrow warmth.* The weight of her trust and the fervent hum of wanting more.

Riggs flips open a case of RFID guest badges. "Task is on track. We've traced the flash-bang serial—mil-surp show from Arizona show last year. Lead is thin, but we'll pull the thread."

"Keep pulling," I grunt.

17:47 — Ballroom main entry. I supervise the crew laying tempered-glass panels over the parquet floor—Camille's idea so the swirling gowns will reflect color like a living kaleidoscope. She appears beside me in paint-dusted jeans, hair swept in a low knot, clipboard in hand.

"How many more vendors?" I ask.

"Just the floral ceiling team—they'll rig the wisteria chandeliers tomorrow." She glances at the new cameras mounted near the chandeliers' anchor points. "You really thought of everything."

I want to tell her I'm thinking of her—always her—but professionalism reins me. "Almost," I say. "We install thermal imagers along the trellis after the floral is set. Any unauthorized heat signature pops on Command."

She nods, lips parting as if to say something more intimate, then shuts them when Anderssen arrives to ask about smoke-machine placement (denied; too many false alarms). I walk the crew through alternate haze options, but Cam's presence at my shoulder hums louder than the drills.

21:08 —A hush settles over the estate. Vendor vans gone, Orange-Team on staggered patrols. Out on the east lawn, Malik's silhouette glides along hedges, rifle slung. I finish logging the day's contractor sign-outs, then force myself to eat a protein bar; it tastes like chalk.

My phone buzzes: **Cam**: *Can't sleep. Come to the studio?*

Adrenaline spikes. I type *On my way*, check with Riggs (northwatch covered), then move.

The carriage-house studio glows low amber. I step in. Cam stands barefoot in one of my black **BRAVO** T-shirts—she must've raided my duffel—shirt hanging mid-thigh, paint streaks on her calves. Her hair is down and wild. She holds a fresh canvas the size of a door.

"I needed white space," she says, breath slightly ragged. "All day I had noise."

"Show me."

She plants the canvas on the easel, then faces me across the drop cloth. "It's blank, Sawyer. Sometimes blank is the scariest thing."

"I know the feeling." I shrug out of my jacket, and roll up my sleeves. "Where do you start?"

"Color first," she whispers.

"Pick one." My voice drops too. "I'll load the palette."

Her gaze flicks to the shelves of tubes, and she chooses a crimson oxide. I squeeze a bead onto the glass, adding ultramarine, and a dab of titanium buff. She dips her fingers straight into the crimson, steps to the canvas, and swipes a diagonal arc—blood-bright slash. Another stroke intersects—blue colliding, bruising purple.

I watch her body flow: foot brace, hip shift, neck arch—every move a silent percussion my pulse accompanies. She finishes a third line, breathing hard, chest rising beneath the borrowed T-shirt that skims curves I'm trying desperately not to stare at.

She turns, her hands red and blue. "Borrow warmth again?"

"Cam." Just her name is a gravity well.

She crosses the drop cloth. Paint-flecked fingers rise to my chest, leaving two smears over my heart. "I tried, but I can't wait till after," she says, voice trembling. "Life's not guaranteed between now and then."

The truth slams home. Bombs teach you that tomorrow can misfire. Protocol or no, I want this now.

I cup her neck. She exhales a broken sound. I lean in, hover a breath from her lips. "Last chance to redraw lines."

She presses up on tiptoe. "Lines are overrated."

I close the distance.

The kiss is molten—nothing hesitant, all pent-up hunger unleashed. She tastes of mint and turpentine and midnight confessions. I angle her back against the canvas. Her paint-wet palms spread on my shoulders, leaving me marked. She gasps when my tongue sweeps her lower lip, then opens on a sweet moan as I deepen the kiss, anchoring one hand at her waist, the other threading into loose waves.

Colors smear where her back grazes the canvas. She hooks a leg behind my knee, and the T-shirt rides up, revealing the smooth plane of her thigh. My self-control riots—days of holding back shredding under the press of her body keen against mine.

But danger still looms, and even as I taste her, some part of me clocks every sound: the creak of rafters, distant footstep of an Orange patrol. I tear my mouth away, breathing hard against her forehead. "Doors locked, cameras covering. Still not enough."

She trails kisses down my jaw, whispering, "We have minutes. I need to feel alive with you."

I grip her hips, rest my forehead to hers. "Alive, yes. Safe, always." My thumb traces the hem of the shirt at her thigh, and she shivers. "And when that bastard's behind bars…"

"Then you won't hold back," she finishes, voice shimmering with promise.

"I'll paint this whole room with us," I vow.

She smiles, presses another lingering kiss—slow, claiming—and I taste hope. When she finally pulls back, eyes lazy with heat, I step away only far enough to scan windows. Clear.

"Come," I murmur, lacing our fingers. "You sleep as I watch."

"No watching tonight," she counters, tugging me toward the villa. "Just us sharing space."

We steal through moonlit corridors to her bedroom. I perform a rapid sweep—closet, bath, balcony. Secure.

She heads into the shower as I remove my paint-stained

shirt. When she comes back in, she sucks in a breath. I suck in a deeper one.

Standing before me is a goddess. All soft curves and deliciously decadent in nothing but a tank and sleep shorts.

Fuck me.

She climbs onto the bed, and extends a hand. I kick off my boots, and remove my holster, then join her, sitting back against the headboard. She crawls into the V of my legs, head on my chest, heartbeat syncing to mine.

"Stay," she breathes.

"Always."

Her fingers trace lazy circles over my sternum. Minutes stretch—not silence but communion. Eventually her breaths lengthen, tension melts, and the weight of her sleep settles.

I watch shadows drift across the ceiling and mark every second I keep her safe. The taste of her still smolders on my lips, an ember I'll guard like the last light on earth. Because yes, lines blurred tonight. But the vow underneath is sharper than ever:

No one reaches her.

And when the gala lights fade and the threat is gone, nothing will keep me from diving into every kaleidoscopic color she's waited to share.

12

Camille

The afternoon sun drifts through the wisteria canopy like liquid apricot, gilding everything in warmth that feels fragile. It's too fragile for the nerves twisting in my gut. Twenty-one hours until the gala. Twenty-one hours until two hundred champagne-slick donors and four hundred glitter-drunk influencers swarm this house like moths around a spotlight.

"To pre-panic or post-panic, that is the question." I mutter it at the sky, then tip the last inch of chardonnay into Vanessa's glass.

She lounges beside me on the teak daybed in a gauzy jade romper, legs stretched, toes painted merlot. "I vote pre," she says, twirling the stem between her fingers. "Panic now so tomorrow you can glide like a swan."

"Swan murder is a felony, Ness."

"Only if they find the body." She clinks her glass against mine. "Cheers to the most stressful soirée this city has ever seen."

We sip. The wine is citrusy with a whisper of honeysuckle. It's like summer in a stem. For a heartbeat I almost forget the weighted lock bolts, the hidden cameras, the operators pacing the tree line.

"So," Vanessa begins, eyes glinting. "Tell me everything about Beard-Mountain."

"Riggs?"

"Obviously. He's silent and broody and looks like he can bench-press my ego."

I laugh. "He's Sawyer's teammate, BRAVO Team's second. Afghanistan vets, apparently. Loves bourbon and dogs. That's all I've gathered."

"Bourbon and dogs? Sold." She sinks deeper into the cushion. "But my girl intuition says the true drama is between you and Captain Discipline."

Heat climbs my cheeks before I can control it. "Sawyer's strictly professional."

"Professional doesn't leave finger-paint hickeys on your neck." Vanessa's grin is wicked. "Relax. I'm kidding. So? Spill."

Sawyer

I toy with the base of my glass. Images flash behind my eyelids. Sawyer's hand cradling my nape, the crush of his mouth, paint smears on his throat. My pulse stumbles.

"Nothing unprofessional," I say. Technically true … if we redefine *nothing*. "He's focused on the gala."

Vanessa snorts. "Focused on *you* more likely." She nudges my knee. "Have you thought about what happens after? When the bad guys are in cuffs and gala confetti's swept?"

"Every waking second." The confession slips out, soft and shivery. "I've never felt so seen. Or so safe."

"Or so turned on," she sings.

"Vanessa!"

She cackles, then sobers. "You deserve safe and steamy. Don't sabotage it."

A wind gust rattles the wisteria leaves, scattering purple petals. I track one drifting onto my thigh. "What if tomorrow goes sideways? What if this person—or people—make their move?"

"Then Sawyer and Beard-Mountain will go full John Wick, and I'll livestream from a tasteful angle." She angles her glass. "Kidding. But honestly, the security here is Fort Knox on steroids."

I glance toward the house. Beyond the French doors I can see one Orange operator—Rae—doing a final walk-through with a tablet. "And yet someone breached twice already."

Vanessa follows my gaze, then lowers her voice. "There's still no leads?"

"The flash-bang traced to a surplus show. Paper stock traced to a specialty boutique, but the sales list was hacked. Hartley's team's cross-referencing Kingsley ex-employees, but nothing concrete."

She sighs. "Any other theories? A jealous ex? A rival artist?"

I think of every critic who's hated my murals, every opportunist who's courted my father's approval only to be turned down. None fit the escalating precision of these attacks.

"Could be someone targeting Dad, using me as leverage," I say. "IPO sharks can be vicious."

Vanessa tilts her head. "Then they'll strike when the media's here—to humiliate him."

"Exactly. Tomorrow's perfect. It's cameras and chaos."

She reaches over, and squeezes my hand. "Then we'll be vigilant and still sparkle." She sits up, eyebrow cocked. "Speaking of sparkle, Sawyer's been circulating like a comet all afternoon, and you haven't ogled him once in ten minutes. Are you broken?"

My lips curve. "He's strip-searching the valet schedule."

"Hot." She drains her glass, and stands. "I'm refilling. You?"

"One more won't hurt." I watch her glide across the patio toward the French doors, hips swaying. The moment she's inside, I exhale, rubbing my temple to quell the adrenaline swirl.

Footsteps crunch behind me. My pulse leaps before I even turn. "Speak of professional devils," I say.

Sawyer steps onto the veranda in slate-gray tactical trousers and a navy polo that fits like temptation tailor-made. Aviators shield his eyes, but I can feel the heat of his focus. "Vendor review complete," he says, voice low, dipping into a register that brushes every nerve ending. "AV crew double-verified credentials. No anomalies."

"Good." I pat the cushion beside me—casual invitation laced with need. "Sit. Take two minutes."

He glances to the door Vanessa disappeared into, then back. Slowly he lowers onto the daybed, boots flat on the decking, forearms resting on his thighs. Close enough for the sleeve of his polo to graze my arm when I breathe deep.

"How's the pulse?" he asks.

"Erratic." I smile. "And yours?"

"Steady." A beat. "Mostly."

The word tangles between us. The veranda, shaded and scented with wisteria, collapses into a bubble of charged air. I want to crawl into his lap, forget fear, but the hum of patrol radios floats from the garden.

"I can't stop thinking about last night," I murmur.

His jaw flexes. "Me either."

"That kiss—"

"Cam." My name is a warning and a caress. "I need you clear tomorrow."

"I'm trying, but you're a walking distraction."

He huffs a low laugh. "You're a masterpiece of distraction."

We lock eyes, and the magnet pulls. I sway, but Vanessa reappears, wine bottle raised. "Corkscrew surrendered willingly!" she announces, halting when she sees Sawyer. "Oh—security huddle?"

Sawyer stands, neutral mask sliding down. "Just briefing Ms. Kingsley." He nods to me, then retreats down the steps, headset already rising to relay orders.

Vanessa plops onto his vacated space. "You could fry eggs on that tension."

Sawyer

"Scrambled," I groan.

She refills our glasses, then leans in. "Okay, Operation ID Psycho: let's brainstorm."

We spend an hour toggling theories. Ex-Kingsley employees: Maybe Dad's former COO, Spencer DeLuna, fired last year for insider leaks. Bitter rival artist: Jasper Haynes, whose mural bid lost to mine downtown. A radical environmental group mad at corporate jets? But nothing fits the precision nor the personal taunts about paint covering blood.

Vanessa sighs. "We need Sherlock."

"I have Sawyer. And a full BRAVO intel team."

"Yes, but you can't make out with Sherlock." She wiggles brows. "Yet."

I grip my glass. "I don't just want a fling, Ness. This feels … big."

Her expression softens. "Then hold on tight."

EDGAR SERVES a light dinner of citrus-herb chicken, quinoa, and grilled peaches. Vanessa chatters about seating charts while Sawyer stands sentinel near the bay window. Every time my fork touches my lips I sense his gaze, a heated sweep. Dessert is skipped, the nerves killing my hunger.

Later in the evening, Vanessa yawns theatrically. "Beauty rest. Tomorrow I need to sparkle like a disco ball." She hugs me, and whispers, "Maybe let Captain Discipline relax too," then sashays out, leaving rose-vanilla perfume in her wake.

Moments later Sawyer appears, silent as dusk. "Vanessa to her suite?"

"Riggs is escorting her to the guest house." I pace before the fireplace. "Everything feels ready but not ready. Like the calm before—"

"Not calm. Controlled." He moves beside me, and grips my shoulders gently. "We've drilled scenarios. You'll shine. We'll keep you safe."

I let my head tip forward onto his chest, breathing in cedar and starch. His heartbeat thrums steady. "Stay again tonight?"

"No place else I'd rather." He lifts my chin. Moonlight slices across his jaw. The need to kiss him claws inside me. I rise on toes—but he stops me with a thumb to my lower lip, gaze scorching.

"After," he whispers. "And when it comes, it will be everything."

Sawyer

The promise sends lightning crackling across skin. I swallow and nod, a chill skating over my shoulders.

SLEEP EVADES ME. Sawyer sits in the chair, reading camera feeds on his tablet, but every so often his eyes flick to me.

I push back the covers. "Come here."

He stands, and steps to the bedside. "Cam…"

"Just a real kiss to keep me brave." My plea trembles. "Then I'll sleep."

He hesitates, then sits on the edge, palm sliding to cup my cheek. The world narrows to the shadowed crease of his lips as he leans down. Soft, at first—just a brush—but I part for him, greedy, and his restraint shreds. His mouth slants over mine, tongue stroking deep in a perfect unhurried glide that draws a whimper from my throat. His hand splays over my ribs, thumb brushing the curve of my breast through my satin cami. I arch, heat pooling.

He breaks away, his voice rough. "Tomorrow." A vow, a threat, a mercy.

I nod, dazed. He tucks me in, kisses my forehead, then returns to the chair—but his smile is feral, and I know dawn can't come fast enough.

Despite nerves, I drift off, cradling the taste of him like a secret talisman. Whatever lurks behind tomorrow's curtain, Sawyer Maddox waits in the wings—wall, door, and soon, if fate is kind, everything in between.

13

Sawyer

Security is a symphony when it finally harmonizes—layers of sensors humming, radios chiming, operators moving like perfectly rehearsed instruments. I've spent forty-eight hours fine-tuning that symphony and now, as dusk settles violet over Saint Pierce, it's showtime.

Floodlights bathe Kingsley House in amber and pearl. The wrought-iron gates—reinforced, magnet-locked—clack open at precisely nineteen hundred. On cue, valet attendants in dove-gray uniforms glide forward. Orange Team patrols the perimeter in staggered overlap, short barrel rifles slung discreetly beneath their jackets, earpieces pulsing steady comm traffic in my ear.

"Command to One," Malik's baritone crackles. "First limo inbound. Credentials match pre-registration. Proceed?"

"Proceed," I answer, adjusting my tux jacket. The black Brioni hides a Kevlar lining—bullet-resistant elegance. Sig rides under my left arm. Micro radio throat mic loops my collar. Show, but with teeth.

The limo glides past manicured topiary, and as it halts, I step forward. The door opens, and Gregory Kingsley emerges—navy tux cut to midwestern broadness, salt-and-pepper hair immaculate, trademark Kingsley tie-pin winking under the floodlight.

He spots my BRAVO badge, and smiles warmly. "Mr. Maddox, I presume."

I nod, and extend a hand. "Good evening, sir. Welcome home."

We shake. His grip is firm, boardroom-tested. "Camille assures me you've turned this place into Fort Knox."

"We prefer 'art-centric fortress,'" I reply. He chuckles. Briefcase in left hand—could hide anything, but I know from pre-check it's his speech notes. Two Kingsley aides exit behind him.

"I appreciate you keeping my daughter safe." His tone drops, genuine. "That mural incident scared the hell out of me."

"We have eyes everywhere tonight. Enjoy yourself."

He nods, steps toward the red-carpeted entry. A camera flash pops. Reporters hover just outside the gate, blocked by barricades. Gregory lifts a courteous hand, then disappears inside.

I exhale, scan feeds on my wrist tablet. The interior ballroom cams show caterers aligning hors d'oeuvres trays while the string quartet tunes. Good.

"Orange check," I murmur. An echo of "clear" sounds from Rae, Anderssen, Malik, Riggs at their posts.

And then, at the top of the grand staircase, she appears.

Camille descends like liquid midnight wrapped in sapphire. The gown hugs her torso, plunges at the back into a waterfall of silk that swishes against each step. Her hair is pinned in an intricate twist, leaving her neck—a delicate line I suddenly crave to taste—bared except for a single diamond drop necklace. Blue satin gloves kiss her elbows. Every flashbulb aims up, but I'm sunk too deep to notice anyone else.

My heart, usually a metronome, misses a beat.

She glances down, finds me by the door, and her smile detonates quietly—private, incendiary. For all my training, I stand rooted as she reaches the marble floor and glides toward me.

"You're supposed to be invisible," she teases, voice soft as the silk brushes the tile.

"Impossible tonight," I say, tone failing to hide the awe. "You're luminous."

She flushes a rose tint. "Professional distance, remember?"

"Respectfully attempting," I murmur.

Gregory reappears, and intercepts his daughter. "Pumpkin," he says, proud grin wide. "You look stunning."

"Dad, the nickname." She cringes good-naturedly, then kisses his cheek. "Everything's ready. AV has your mic."

He nods. "Keep her in that spotlight and off the tabloids, hm?"

"We'll handle it."

As Gregory mingles, Cam's gaze returns to me. For a sliver of a moment, the party noise recedes, and we just breathe each other's air.

Rae's voice interrupts. "Ingress gate secure, Phase Two donors arriving."

Duty first. I incline my head. "Time to shine. I'm two steps away if you need anything."

She touches my forearm through my tux—two heartbeats, then she's gone, floating into the throng.

FROM MY VANTAGE near a pillar draped in orchids, I track Cam's every move. She greets donors, laughs with the mayor, poses beside the community mural projected across a thirty-foot screen. Blue gown fans as she gestures, each movement a brushstroke come alive.

Riggs sidles up, sipping club soda. "Copycat shooter nowhere in sight."

"Let's keep it that way." I flick to the west-wing feed—Malik patrolling the caterer corridor—then to the rooftop drone. Thermal shows only authorized personnel.

Music swells—string quartet shifting to a modern arrangement of "Can't Help Falling in Love." Cam finishes greeting the last executive, then steps to the dance floor with graceful hesitation. Her eyes search and find me.

Dance with me? the look says.

Professional? Not even close. But we built this fortress so she can live. Tonight, living means dancing with the man who can't stop wanting her.

I approach, comms crackling low: "Riggs, Malik, Rae, maintain visual."

Cam offers her gloved hand. I take it, the satin on my calloused skin feels electric. We step into the waltz.

"I thought you didn't dance," she murmurs, smiling up.

"I assess threats," I say, guiding her in a smooth box turn. "Right now the only threat is how stunning you are."

Color blooms across her cheeks. "Flattery might be unprofessional."

"Then fire me tomorrow." I spin her, and the gown arcs like a comet trail. Eyes follow us—media whispers, donors intrigued—but my world is this measured swirl of blue silk and the scent of her gardenia perfume.

Halfway through the song, Rae's voice cuts in: "Command, we have a possible in the north hedge—heat signature, stationary, looks like tech kit."

I stiffen, pulse spiking, but keep my smile for onlookers. "Copy. Riggs intercept silently. I retain asset."

Cam feels my tension. "What is it?" she whispers.

"Nothing you need to worry about." I pivot us away from the cameras toward a darker corner. "Smile for the crowd."

She does, though her fingers tighten on my shoulder.

"Riggs, status?" I murmur.

"False alarm—ground squirrel sitting on warm transformer," he returns. Relief flicks. "Tell your squirrel security deposit due."

I exhale, easing. The waltz ends, and applause rises. Cam curtsies. I bow. Cameras flash.

As we exit the floor, Hartley (out of uniform in a simple tux) greets Cam, compliments the mural, nods to me with knowing respect. His plainclothes detectives are spread around.

Sawyer

A while later, Gregory presents a scholarship fund, and bidders raise paddles. Cam stands side-stage, anxious but radiant. Her father squeezes her hand after the gavel drops on the final painting for $850,000. She beams and I forget how to breathe.

Rae reports zero anomalies. Media clamor outside the press zone, but crowd flow remains orderly. My shoulders loosen—maybe the threat burned itself out.

Guests head to the lawn marquee for dessert. I guide Cam along the lantern-lit path. Fire pits flicker, violins play softer as the champagne flows.

"You did it," I say low. "No drama."

"Couldn't have without you." Her eyes shine, emotion heavy. "Sawyer, thank you—"

An urgent hiss in my ear. "One to Command—Geiger anomaly in cellar corridor. Audible ticking. I repeat: ticking source unknown."

Ice water sluices through my veins.

"Riggs, intercept. Malik block cellar stair. Evac quiet."

Cam notices my body go rigid. "Sawyer?"

I grip her elbow, smile wide for nearby guests, and whisper, "We have to move, right now."

She pales but nods. I steer her behind the dessert tent, away from crowd eyes. Over comm, I say, "Riggs?"

"Object located behind catering crates. Cylindrical, capped, analog timer—two minutes on clock."

My worst nightmare. "Do not touch. Establish blast perimeter ten meters. Evac all staff."

Cam's hand clutches my coat. "Is it a *bomb*?" Her voice cracks on the last word.

"Likely improvised device." Calm voice, shaking soul. "I've got this."

I call Rae to keep patrons confined to the lawn. Anderssen reroutes valet flow. Malik clears the east wing. In less than thirty seconds an invisible cordon forms—guests oblivious under twinkle lights.

I turn to Cam. "Go with Rae to the command trailer."

Her lips tremble, but her chin lifts. "Not a chance. I want to be with you."

"No," I say, clutching both her shoulders, my eyes boring into hers.

"What are you going to do?"

I step close, erasing inches. "I'm going to assess the bomb, and then diffuse it."

Her eyes blow wide. "I…uh, but…what if…" she doesn't finish her thought, and I won't let her because I do something highly unprofessional, I lean in, capturing her lips with mine. I kiss her like my soul's on fire. I step back, brush a thumb down her cheek, then sprint.

I HEAD INTO THE CELLAR, and check to make sure Rae has Camille.

Riggs crouches behind a steel prep table flipped as makeshift cover. The device sits three meters ahead. A silver thermos-like cylinder strapped with duct tape, analog kitchen timer whirring down from ninety seconds. Classic intimidation build—simple but lethal in close quarters.

"Blocked door swing," Riggs whispers. "I can't guarantee a full seal from up top."

"Get clear," I order, scanning components. No wires leading away, no shimmer of mercury tilt. Likely a pipe bomb with black-powder main charge, maybe nails. Timer leads into spring striker. Basic.

"Time?" Riggs asks.

"Eight-eight." I pop my multitool. If I move the striker plate sideways one millimeter, I can wedge a utensil—wooden spoon—to hold the spring. But if they rigged an anti-tamper, we're dust.

No choice.

I exhale, slip to my knees. Voices crackle in my ear—Malik establishing external evac—but my focus tunnels.

Seven-four seconds.

I unscrew the thermos lid—no anti-tamper beep. Good. Inside, a homemade striker rig, nails taped around inner walls. I slide the tool under the striker bar, wedge and the spring compresses.

Sixteen seconds.

Hold. My hands are steady—muscle memory from deserts and dirt roads of Kandahar. I clip wires from timer to igniter, and sever the current.

Timer ticks uselessly.

And then there's silence.

I exhale once, long. Sweat drips down my spine. "Device disarmed. Request bomb squad for removal."

Comm erupts in relief.

I stand, my legs rubber. Riggs slaps my shoulder. "You're still the best damn EOD I know."

"Let's not test that again."

CAM BURSTS in as soon as Rae opens the door, eyes wet but blazing. "Sawyer!" She throws her arms around my neck, heedless of bomb sweat and talc dust. I hold her hard.

Sawyer

"Neutralized," I whisper into her hair.

She trembles. "I was watching on the cameras. Rae and I both watched. You were so," she breathes in deep, "methodical."

"I had a job to do." I keep a hold of her.

She gazes into my eyes. "Who leaves a bomb at a charity gala?"

"Someone with a vendetta and knowledge of the layout." I pull back, and tilt her face. "We'll find them."

Her hands cup my jaw, eyes bright. "Don't ever do that alone."

"It's what I do."

"It's who you are," she corrects. Then, softer, "It's why I …" She trails off but I know. I press our foreheads together.

Behind us, Rae coughs discreetly. "What's next, Boss?"

I draw a breath, keeping Cam tucked close. "Next? We end this. Tonight proved an escalation. Tomorrow we hunt."

14

Camille

I replay the cellar feed so many times the image blurs—Sawyer, tux jacket shed, gloves on, kneeling before a silver bomb ticking down our destruction. He doesn't flinch when the timer clicks below thirty. He merely breathes, steady and sure, hands moving with lethal grace. One clip, one twist, and the second hand stops. A war fought in murmurs and micro-movements. A war he wins for me.

The recording ends. My lungs ache as if I'd held the bomb myself. All evening I greeted donors and thanked dignitaries, but my mind remained six feet underground, ticking toward ruin with him. Sexy—and terrifying—that the man who guarded my brushstrokes could disarm death while still smelling faintly of gun oil and midnight rain.

A soft knock draws me from the monitor glow. My bedroom door creaks open, and Sawyer steps in, hair damp from a quick shower, black t-shirt untucked. Moonlight frames him like a storm given shape. I rise from the desk before thought can intervene.

"Bomb squad's hauled the device," he says, voice low. "Guests will never know."

I swallow the fist of fear clawing my throat. "You could've died."

"Could have," he agrees, crossing to me. "Didn't."

His calm frays my composure. I rush forward, fists balling in his shirt. "What if you hadn't? One wrong wire—" My voice cracks. "I can't lose you."

He folds me against his chest, chin resting atop my head. His heartbeat—steady even now—echoes through my ribs. "Not planning on going anywhere."

I lean back, and search his eyes. "Stay tonight. Please."

He brushes a curl from my cheek. "I'll always say yes to you." The promise vibrates deeper than a vow.

Heat blooms. I tip my face, capturing his mouth. The kiss is hungry. Indecent. It's no polite brush, but more like a claiming. He answers in kind, hands sliding down my spine, gathering the satin of my gown until my body molds to the hard planes of his. I gasp as his tongue coaxes mine, teasing and tasting.

"Cam," he rasps against my lips, "tell me to stop if—"

"Don't you dare," I breathe, threading my fingers through his hair. I tug lightly, and a groan rumbles in his chest, thrilling me. His palms splay over my hips, drawing me closer, until not even air fits between us.

We stumble toward the bed, mouths never parting. He sits first, pulling me astride his lap. The split of my gown pools around us like sapphire waves. I cradle his jaw, kissing him slow and deep. He answers with reverence, as though mapping every contour to memory.

His hands glide up my back, finding the hidden zipper. He hesitates—granting me the choice. I whisper "yes," and the gown loosens, sliding off one shoulder. His lips follow the path, pressing fire along my exposed skin. I arch, my fingers digging into his shoulders.

When he lifts his head, pupils blown, breath ragged, I see battlefields and sunsets and every line he's drawn finally erased. He cups my face. "You are color and oxygen."

"And you're my shield," I whisper, kissing the corner of his smile.

I guide him down onto the pillows as the moonlight strokes the angles of his face. Our mouths meet again—slow, then faster, matching the gallop of our heartbeats. His hands roam with aching care, as if memorizing sacred art. I let the gown fall completely, baring silk and skin, and his breath hitches—a sound of wonder that steals mine.

Sawyer

We tumble sideways, laughter catching on our mouths, kisses turning greedy and then soft, urgent and tender in the same breath. The sheets caress my shoulder blades; his chest is heat and cedar, the steady drum of his heart against mine. When his fingertips skim the curve of my thigh, a shiver sparks low and bright—I arch into his touch, shameless, silently asking for more.

He pauses, searching my face like he's reading a map he already knows by heart. I hold his gaze and let yes flood every inch of me—chin tipped up, breath trembling, hand guiding his wrist higher. Consent isn't a word; it's a pulse thudding in my throat, in the press of my palm over his.

The last sliver of restraint slips. "I need you with every cell of my body," he rasps, voice rough velvet.

"I feel exactly the same," I whisper, and it's the truest thing I've ever said.

His mouth crooks into a sinful smirk as his fingers find fabric and peel it away. Mine are just as greedy—buttons, buckles, the warm give of his skin under my hands. Clothes scatter with little gasps and clinks, and suddenly there is only heat and the delicious shock of bare everywhere. We pause—just five reverent seconds—stretched out, drinking each other in like a masterpiece revealed.

God. He is carved from light and shadow—clean lines, the slope of his shoulders, the tight plane of his abdomen, those strong thighs braced like promise. He's a study in sculpted symmetry and barely leashed hunger, and the longer I stare the harder it is to remember how to breathe. My mouth actually parts. My fingers trace down the path my eyes took, slow and worshipful, and he shudders under the touch, that wicked smile softening at the edges as if my awe is undoing him.

"Come here, Cam," he murmurs.

I crawl over him, straddling his hips, palms splayed on that perfect chest, and lower myself over his thick hardness. My voice is a sigh against his lips. "Tell me when to stop."

"Never," he says, and I swallow the word with a kiss, tasting promise and heat as I roll my hips—showing him exactly how ready I am, how completely I want him. The room blurs; the world tilts to just us; and the only rhythm I know is the pant of his breath and the way he melts when I touch him like he's the only work of art I'll ever want to make.

"You're perfect," I whisper to him, running my nails over the broad muscles of his chest, my body riding him up and down, over and over again.

"That's it, Cam, *fuck*..."

The rough, low gravel of his voice—need braided into every syllable—lights me up; heat surges through me and my hips quicken on instinct, rocking harder to match the hunger he breathes into the dim room.

He grips my hips, moving north toward my breasts as he pitches forward, his mouth covering my nipple. He repositions us, to where I'm flat on my back, him on top of me. He enters me in one quick thrust, both of us stilling once he's all the way inside.

"Fuck, Cam… you feel so *fucking* good." His need is thick in his voice.

I gaze into his gray eyes, the color mesmerizing me. "Please don't ever stop."

He smoothes a hand over my hair, his eyes locking onto mine as he thrusts his hips forward. "*Never.*"

Heat unfurls under my sternum, spreading outward in slow, pulsing waves at the way he holds me—hands firm at my hips, touch sure and reverent, like he's staking a claim he intends to keep. His breath ghosts my ear, our rhythm syncing until the room blurs and all I feel is the steady insistence of us. It's intoxicating, this sense that he's nowhere else and never will be, that we're suspended in a pocket of time made just for two. I don't want the moment to thin or spill; I want to stretch it wide, memorize every breath and shiver, and live right here where his touch says *stay*. I would press a pin in this second and keep it forever.

He keeps moving inside me, slow and unhurried at first, and then his tempo picks up. He presses his forehead against mine, and our breaths become mingled together as things escalate.

"Take all of me. I'm yours," he whispers into my mouth and I spread my legs even farther, letting him slip deeper inside me. "Are you on the pill?"

I smirk. "Kind of late for the birth control talk, isn't it?"

He growls. "Cam, tell me."

I gaze into his eyes, memorizing him. "Yes, I'm on the pill." My body builds closer to that pivotal moment. Toward the release we're both chasing. "I'm so close." I grip onto him tighter.

He bucks away on top of me, his body solid and ... *perfect*. "Come all over me, Cam. I've got you." And I believe him.

This man has had me since day one. Since I first laid eyes on him. He's had me. Hook, line, and sinker.

"Don't ever let go," I tell him, my body so dang close. "*Sawyer*," I say his name like a prayer as my body detonates. "Ah, Sawyer," I shout and his grip on me tightens.

"Give it to me, Cam. I've got you."

I don't stop. My body doesn't slow down as a tsunami of emotions slam into my chest all at once. "Sawyer," now his name comes out as a curse. "Fuck me," I whisper as my body starts the downward slope.

He takes my words as an invitation to let loose. He bucks and fucks. He thrusts into me harder than before. He uses me as he seeks out his own release. And I enjoy every second of it. "You're *fucking* gorgeous," he says between pumps of his dick. "So *fucking* pretty."

I soak in his praise like heat after a winter plunge, each honeyed word pouring over me until my skin prickles and my muscles go loose and heavy. The warmth spreads from my chest to my fingers and toes, a slow, sweet tide that leaves me boneless and bright, even as my lungs still chase breath. I'm wrung out and trembling, yet every nerve is lit—vibrating with the echo of his voice, the thrum of my pulse, the lingering spark of every place his hands have been.

And then he kisses me. A full, soul-searing kiss that owns me in every sense of the word. His body stills slightly as his release hits him. He grips tight…then lets loose. Each pump of his hips slams into me, his dick pulsing as his release floods inside me. "You're everything," he whispers. "*Every-fucking-thing.*"

15

Sawyer

Morning should smell like fresh espresso and lemon polish, but the Kingsley House reeks of the stale aftermath of a gala. Orange Team operators pace the grounds in daylight patrols. A mobile forensics van idles by the portico, CSU techs collecting one last round of any evidence they can find before shipping it upriver to Quantico.

Fortresses, it turns out, can bleed.

I rub my sternum—phantom ache where Cam's heartbeat slept against mine only hours ago. The memory of her satin skin, her breathy moans still ghost across my senses like aftershocks. Focus, Maddox. You promised her the world at dawn. First you have to keep her alive to see the sunset.

Rae hands me her overnight incident log as we stride toward the command trailer. "Drone captured a black

SUV circling the perimeter at oh-three-twenty. No plates. Disappeared west on Cedar."

"Forward footage to Hartley." I flip pages. "Any chatter on police frequencies?"

She grimaces. "Media leak. KRX News aired *'Heiress Horror: Bomb at Kingsley Charity Gala.'* They're speculating internal sabotage."

"Perfect." I toss the packet on the desk as we step inside. Screens bloom with live feeds; headlines crawl across one monitor:

Insider Tips FBI to Kingsley Bomb!

Charity Catastrophe: Is the Blue Princess a Target?

Somewhere, someone is feeding the vultures.

"Malik," I bark through comms, "pull today's domestic staff roster. Cross-check against comms logs. I want to know who had phone access last night after the lockdown."

"On it," he replies.

Riggs enters carrying two coffees and an expression that says *intervention*. He slides a cup my way. "Double espresso. Figured you'd need intravenous."

I grunt thanks, take a scalding swallow—bitterness matches the acid in my gut. Riggs leans back against a gear case, arms folded. "You heading off a cliff, brother."

"Cliff looks like?"

"Emotional free-fall. Eyes glazed. No sleep. And…" He gestures vaguely to my torso. "Paint smudges?"

I glance down. A faint streak of cobalt blue arcs across my black shirt—Cam's mark from when our bodies collided into dawn. Heat flicks under my collar even as adrenaline spikes. "Working case," I say.

"Uh-huh." He studies me. "You love her?"

The question detonates in my chest. "Don't go there."

"Too late—you're already *there*. Just make sure your heart doesn't override the mission." He turns serious. "Whoever planted that bomb knew our sensor grid, Sawyer. This isn't a star-struck fan. It's strategic."

"I know." I rake a hand through my hair. "We're missing a link—someone inside feeding intel. We lock tighter, we flush them out."

Before Riggs can push further, my phone buzzes with Gregory Kingsley's number. I pick up. "Sir?"

"Mr. Maddox. Meet me in the west library." The tone brooks no delay.

I hand the coffee back to Riggs and head out.

07:35 — West Library

Sawyer

Sunlight slants across rows of rare first editions. Gregory stands at the window, phone in one hand, Wall Street Journal in the other. Headlines about the bomb glare from the business section.

He turns, eyes bloodshot behind rimless glasses. "I trusted this house was secure. Yet a device nearly killed my donors—and my daughter."

A jab of guilt lands square. "We neutralized the threat. No casualties."

"But what about next time?" He paces. "Camille won't leave. She thinks bravery and stubbornness are synonyms. I need options."

"Options?" I echo.

"Relocation. A safe house. Or overseas—she loves the Amalfi studio my wife left her. Could you escort her there until this blows over?" His voice trembles at *wife*, grief simmering fresh.

I fold my hands behind my back in a professional stance. "She's safest under the net we control. But if you order it, I'll implement extraction protocols."

He sighs, rubbing his temples. "She'll fight me. Says the community needs her here, painting over darkness. I admire that—but I'd trade every Kingsley share to keep her heart beating."

His desperation mirrors my own silent terror from last night. I step closer. "Mr. Kingsley, I have feelings for your daughter." The admission crashes out before caution can muzzle it. "But that won't cloud my judgment. If extraction becomes necessary, I'll do it."

He studies me, surprise flickering into something like acceptance. "You risked your life for her already. Perhaps that qualifies you more than most." He exhales. "Press conference in an hour. Statement's being drafted. Public wants reassurance and the shareholders want blood. Just keep my girl… whole."

He leaves with the paper rolled tight like a baton. The door clicks shut, reverberations jangling my bones.

Back in Command, Orange-Team has flagged two suspicious staff calls; Hartley is already subpoenaing tower logs. But leaks spread like fissures. TMZ drone footage pops up on TikTok—Kingsley House lit by police strobes, bomb squad hauling a canister. The narrative spirals unchecked.

I phone Dean.

He answers on the first ring. "Dog and pony show going sideways?"

"Media breach. Strategic infiltration. Kingsley wants relocation. I'm leaning toward extraction until we ID the mole."

Dean exhales. "Pulling her mid-crisis may embolden the attacker, but public frenzy compromises perimeter."

"So we go dark. Off-grid property west of Saint Pierce, near Wolfsridge Canyon. In the mountains. Orange-Team can re-fortify in twelve hours."

"Agree. Who compromises command here?"

"Riggs stays onsite with Malik to liaise with PD. Rae, Anderssen on convoy with me and Cam."

"Do it fast, low-vis. And Sawyer—cut emotional entanglement loose until thread's snipped. Operatives in love bleed mistakes."

"Who says I'm in love? Did you talk to Riggs?" Motherfucker.

"Just stay clear."

My grip tightens on the phone. "Copy." But love isn't a switch I can flick.

09:10 — **Cam's studio**

She's at the easel, bare feet, Sawyer-T-shirt, wielding a palette knife like a saber. A new canvas—storm clouds swirling cobalt and ember. She turns, reading urgency in my stride.

"What happened?"

"Press leaked the bomb story. Paparazzi will swarm. Your father's worried."

She wipes paint on a rag. "He wants to hide me."

"He wants you alive." I step close, lowering my voice. "I propose a temporary relocation. Isolated safe house, new sensor grid. 48-hour blackout until we track the mole."

Her eyes search mine—fear, frustration, and a small flicker of hope. "Will you be there?"

"Every second."

She exhales, her shoulders dropping. "Then yes."

I stroke her paint-dusty cheek. "Pack essentials—no digital devices. We roll in ninety."

"Tell me you'll come back for my paints," she jokes weakly.

"I'll buy every tube in Wolfsridge Canyon."

She smiles, brave. I want to kiss her, to steal one slice of calm before the storm, but footsteps clack.

Vanessa.

"Morning drama or afternoon?" Vanessa asks, sipping iced coffee.

"More like relocation," Cam answers, slipping into logistics.

Vanessa's brows lift but she nods. "Where?"

"Undisclosed," I say.

She salutes with her straw. "He's getting hotter the bossier he gets," she whispers to Cam, earning an eye roll.

11:05 — Motor court

Three black SUVs idle. Rae drives lead, Anderssen tail. I stand beside Cam at the car door, scanning press vans staking out beyond the gate. A Helicopter thumps overhead as a few drones whine.

Riggs jogs over. "PD staging decoy convoy south. Should draw paparazzi."

"Good." I draw Cam's hand to my heart. "Ready?"

"I think so." She slips into the SUV.

Before I round to the driver's seat, Riggs grasps my forearm. "You know what you're doing?"

"Keeping her breathing."

His gaze digs. He nods once, then turns to marshal decoys.

I slide in. Cam links her fingers with mine on the console. Her pulse thrums—but there's no fear. There's only trust.

As we roll through the gates, flashes explode against tinted glass. Media screams questions. My phone buzzes. A text pops on screen:

YOU CAN RUN, BLUE PRINCESS. THE CANVAS IS EVERYWHERE. LET'S ADD MORE RED.

Attached there's a photo of Cam and me dancing last night, crosshairs drawn over our joined hands.

Rage sears. I lock the screen, my thumb forking my shoulder strap. Cam sees, her jaw tightening but she stays composed.

"We'll find them," she whispers.

Glass reflects determination in her hazel eyes, matching my own. The game isn't over; it's escalating. But we're not playing defense anymore. We're bait—and we know it. The difference? This time the hunter faces a shield forged of vigilance, fury, and a love I no longer bother denying.

Let them come.

16

Camille

The mountains rise out of nowhere—jagged silhouettes against a bruised-lavender sky—and I realize I've never truly seen night until now. No city glow, no highway glare. Just a velvet hush pricked with stars and the low purr of our convoy weaving up a switchback ridge that feels halfway to the moon. It's both beautiful and unsettling: beauty because the air smells like woodsmoke and pine sap, unsettling because the blackness presses so thick it could hide anything.

Sawyer said the safe house is "quiet," but the word feels hilariously inadequate when the gates finally loom into the headlights. Twelve feet of reinforced wrought iron, capped with discreet razor wire, slide inward on whisper-silent hydraulics. Beyond, twin beams sweep the drive in a lazy X—motion-tracking floodlights.

"Welcome to Bastion," Sawyer says from the driver's seat, voice a soothing rumble in the dark. He's been calm the entire three-hour drive, but that calm is bulletproof Kevlar stretched over a soul currently set to *siege mode*. I can feel the tension in the way he grips the wheel, a white-knuckle promise that this place will hold.

Rae's SUV turns off down a graveled spur leading to a small A-frame with a wide veranda—the security house. Anderssen flashes his high beams twice.

"What does that mean?" I ask.

"Means all clear and he's moving to watch the perimeter," Sawyer's voice is smooth and controlled.

"All that from two flashes of light?"

Sawyer eyes me with a quick smile. "Yeah."

Then he kills his engine. Their shadows flit across the porch, rifles slung, night-vision goggles lowering. I briefly wonder what sort of neighborly welcome the local wildlife will receive from them.

Our own vehicle climbs another hundred yards to the main residence. It's a modern glass-and-stone structure perched on a rocky ledge, as if an architect decided to sculpt safety from granite. Floor-to-ceiling windows face the valley, but privacy screens already tint the glass. At the top of the driveway, Sawyer taps a code into an inconspicuous panel and the garage yawns open. We

Sawyer

glide inside, the sound of the engine echoing off concrete.

For several heartbeats, silence reigns—then doors thunk, and I follow him into an airlock-style foyer. Biometric reader glows blue before accepting his thumbprint and voice. The heavy bolt slides. We're inside.

The security brief he rattles off as we tour is equal parts impressive and alarming:

- **Thermal perimeter grid**—invisible beams that trip silent alarms before anything organic gets within 200 feet.
- **Steel shutters** hidden in the walls, able to deploy over every pane of glass in under seven seconds.
- **Panic room** tunneled into the mountain, stocked for a week.
- **Faraday cage office** for secure comms and evidence storage.
- **Backup generator** capable of powering a small village.

The house itself is sleek—charcoal slate floors, raw cedar beams, minimalist furniture in dove-gray suede. A stone fireplace anchors the living room, currently dark but stacked with logs. Every line, every texture feels curated to soothe. Yet it also whispers *safe* in a way my childhood mansion never managed.

Sawyer's arm circles my waist as he points out motion detector panels and the coded lock on the wine cellar. He smells like the cedar beams—a scent I'm fast associating with home.

"You built this?" I ask.

"Dean did. Company asset." He brushes a strand of hair behind my ear, his hand warm against my skin. "Few people know it exists."

"Can it really stop whoever's hunting me?"

"Yes," he says. "But I'm the redundancy plan."

He turns me gently, so I face him. The glow from recessed spotlights paints half his face gold, the other half night. "It ends here, Cam. We'll identify them, and then you'll be free to paint your whole damn city."

His certainty wraps around me like the thickest wool blanket. But I still ask the question I haven't dared voice: "And afterward? When you're not charged with babysitting me?"

He steps closer, his heat radiating everywhere. "Afterward starts tonight."

The words pulse through me, lighting every nerve. I slide my hands up his chest—silk shirt over granite muscle—and feel his breath hitch. My own breathing stutters, but I push ahead. "Show me the rest?"

Sawyer

His smile is slow, dangerous. "Master suite," he says, pressing a wall plate that reveals a hidden corridor. Cool air strokes my ankles as we descend three steps into a wing suspended over darkness. Across the glass wall, the valley yawns, scattered with pinpricks of distant cabin lights. It feels as though we're drifting above the world.

The bedroom itself is wider than my entire Manhattan studio rental from college. A platform bed faces the window, the fireplace opposite, and a thick ivory rug begging for bare feet. The bedspread is charcoal linen, rumpled like storm clouds.

Sawyer sets my overnight duffel on a bench, then palms a tablet on the nightstand. "Shutters, set privacy." A hush of motorized steel slides over the window, leaving us in a warm lamplight. My pulse thrums louder than the motors.

He moves to the sideboard, producing two tumblers and a bottle of single-malt. "One finger or two?"

I lean against a cedar post, fighting a quiver that has nothing to do with the chill. "Two."

He pours, passes a glass, and clinks his with mine. The liquor burns honey-peach then settles with an oak finish—liquid courage for a woman who nearly lost everything. I set the glass down half-empty.

"I'm still wearing your T-shirt," I murmur. A smile tugs my mouth. "It feels… protective."

"The shirt can stay," he says, stepping in until his knees brush mine. "But everything underneath…" His hands slide up the hem, warm palms cupping my waist. Sparks fly.

"Approved," I breathe against his lips.

We meet midway—a kiss that begins gentle but segues instantly to hungry. The taste of scotch and adrenaline linger. His hands skim my ribcage, his fingertips mapping. He teases the shirt higher, knuckles brushing against my satin panties. I whimper. He groans, deep and raw.

My fingers find the first button of his shirt—*flick, flick*—exposing heated skin and the scattering of scars he never speaks about. I kiss one pale slash, and feel him tremble.

"Cam," he rasps, tugging my shirt off in a single glide. The satin panties remain, but the rest of me shivers naked under his heated gaze. He stares as if cataloging every brushstroke—appreciation that is almost worship, never ownership. It thrills me in a way I've never felt before.

He cups my face, kisses me slower, like a fine wine tasting. I melt against him, palms roaming his torso, down the slope of his abs to the top button of his pants. He intercepts my hand, eyes sparking. "Bed, first," he growls. It's a playful command that shoots straight to my core.

We tumble onto the mattress, laughter tangled with moans. He props over me, arms bracketing my head, studying me like I'm the final fuse he must cut just right. Then his mouth trails down my throat, over my collarbone, to the heavy ache of my breast. His tongue flicks over my pebbled nipple, his hand cupping the other, and my back arches off the sheets.

I explore him too. His shoulder blade ridges, a bullet scar along his flank, each discovered with lips and fingertips. He mutters half-sworn promises against my skin. *Don't stop. You own me. Never leave.* Each vow counters the fear that has dogged me since the first threat note.

When he finally divests the last barrier—silk sliding, trousers kicked away—the world shrinks to heat and breath and the way we fit together perfectly, like two halves realigning.

"You handle my cock like such a good girl, Cam." He sinks into me with exquisite slowness, and the hush that follows isn't silence; it's a chord finally resolving.

The mountains could fall, and I would barely notice.

We move together, rhythm guided by instinct and the deep hum of shared adrenaline. I clutch his shoulders, nails scoring lightly. He groans, thrusts deeper. I gasp, meeting him with rising abandon. Each glide is a brushstroke, layering color onto canvas until the picture bursts in brilliance—my release, his, mingling in a wild crescendo that leaves us trembling, panting, clinging.

After, he doesn't roll away. Instead, he gathers me close, my cheek to his chest. Our breaths sync with the distant hush of pines swaying outside steel shutters.

"I told your father I'd keep you whole," he murmurs, fingers tracing lazy spirals on my arm. "I intend to keep that vow."

"My father worries about stock prices," I mumble into his skin. "I worry about you running into bombs for me. Seems lopsided."

He chuckles, a rumble under my ear. "Bomb defusing is easier than resisting you."

I smile, pressing a kiss to the sternum scratch I left earlier. "We have forty-eight hours before we head back. How do we spend them?"

"Layering defenses. Loving you. Not necessarily in that order."

The word *love* slips so naturally it stuns me. I lift my head, search his face. No flinch. No back-pedal. Just truth shining in those gray eyes.

I tuck closer, letting his heartbeat lull me. Tomorrow will bring forensic calls, suspect lists, maybe another threat. But tonight, inside steel-sealed walls on a lonely mountaintop, I finally feel like the attack dog at my side and the tempest in my chest are on the same side.

And that, I decide as sleep steals me, is a masterpiece worth any fight.

17

Sawyer

08:04 — Safe-house rec room

Morning sun cuts through clerestory windows, scattering trapezoids of light across the padded floor. Camille bounces on her bare toes in black yoga pants and my charcoal **BRAVO** tee tied at the back, determined to look fierce even with cobalt streaks still ghosting her forearm. She stretches her wrists, watching me set a metronome pulse on the smart speaker—steady, not frantic.

"Self-defense 101," I say, motioning her to the center mat. "Goal isn't to trade blows. It's to break contact and run."

"Run?" She shakes her head, braid loosening. "That's anticlimactic."

"Survival usually is." I demonstrate a basic stance—feet triangular, weight on the balls of my feet. "Show me."

She mirrors with surprising accuracy. "Like this?"

I nod my approval. "First move is the wrist release. Predator grabs your arm? Rotate toward the thumb, and yank free. Strike soft tissue, and then retreat." I reach gently, clasp her right wrist. Her pulse flutters against my fingers—impossibly distracting, but I lock focus. "Ready?"

She inhales, rotates, yanks, then snaps her elbow down—textbook. She springs back, eyes bright. "Again!"

We cycle through variations: single-hand choke defense, knee strike to groin, heel stomp to instep. Each repetition she grows more confident, laughter slipping through grunts.

After a combo that ends with her knee nearly grazing my abdomen, she backs off, panting. "How'd I do?"

I wipe a bead of sweat from her brow with my thumb. "If I were the perp, I'd rethink life choices."

She grins. Then—without warning—lunges, hooks my dominant wrist, and executes the thumb-break release perfectly. I let it happen, half proud, half aroused. She skips away, raising her fists in mock triumph.

"Unexpected attack," she taunts.

"Solid tactic," I admit. "Except you forgot the retreat."

Two strides and I catch her waist, spinning her until her back kisses the padded wall. She laughs breathlessly. Our faces hover inches apart, heat pulsing. I want to kiss her, but the comm in my ear crackles.

"Anderssen to One. Morning sweep complete. Thermal clear, seismic negative; drones on loop."

"Copy," I reply, not moving from Cam's stare. "Status green."

Cam taps the radio bud on my collar, playful. "Tell him I almost neutralized you."

"Fifty-fifty," I murmur, brushing a stray hair from her cheek. She knocks my hand playfully, hearts still thudding.

Rae's voice chimes in next. "Kitchen perimeter set. I made breakfast burritos. Get them before Anderssen inhales the tray."

Cam's eyes light. "Survival fuel."

09:12 — Kitchen island

Rae leans against the counter, pink buzz-cut poking from a baseball cap that reads *Trust But Verify*. Anderssen towers nearby, halfway through a burrito the size of his forearm.

"How's our ninja in training?" Rae asks as Cam reaches for salsa.

"Deadly," I say. "Consider yourselves warned."

Cam raises her foil-wrapped feast in salute. "You guys sure eat like mercenaries."

"Calories equal tactics," Anderssen mumbles around eggs and chorizo.

We debrief overnight sensor logs. Nothing breached. The black SUV never returned to the Kingsley House. Live feeds scroll across a wall-mounted monitor—pine swaying, a deer nibbling brush at the fence line. Idyllic calm.

Still, my shoulders ride a little too high; last night's text crosshairs etched a permanent brand.

Cam nudges me with her hip, whispering, "Your brow is doing that storm-cloud thing."

"Thinking." I stuff the unease down, and flash a reassuring half-smile.

THE SUN CLIMBS high in the sky. We decide on a short hike—recon disguised as a nature stroll. Rae remains at command. Anderssen patrols the southern ridge. I guide Cam along a switchback path edged by granite outcrops and moss plush enough to paint with. The air smells of sun-baked pine needles.

"Have you ever been off-grid this long?" I ask.

"Only at artist retreats, but those had Wi-Fi. This is… primal." She tips her head back, eyes closed, breathing deeply. "Do you ever miss combat?"

Sawyer

"Not combat. Purpose." I flick a pebble off the trail. "I thought BRAVO filled that void, until you."

She stops walking and studies me. "I'm purpose?"

"More like meaning." The confession slips out, raw.

She rests a hand on my chest, thumb rubbing the spread-eagle stitching on my Henley. "You're mine, too. Meaning, I mean."

Branches rustle overhead, but the world stills. I tuck a curl behind her ear. "We'll end this. Then you can paint without barricades."

"And you'll watch without an earpiece," she hopes aloud.

"From your studio floor, coffee in hand." I smile. "Maybe shirtless. For inspiration."

She laughs, cheeks pink. "Deal."

We crest a knoll overlooking a glassy lake. Reflections ripple silver. Cam snaps a mental picture. I know because her fingers twitch as if holding a brush. She whispers, "So many blues."

Standing behind her, I wrap my arms around her stomach, my chin resting on her shoulder. "We'll capture it for the mural you'll finish."

She covers my forearms with her hands, and for a breath everything is okay.

Until Rae's voice breaks in: "All stations, be advised—satellite ping shows media helicopters leaving Saint Pierce, vector unknown. Possible press hunt."

Cam stiffens. I squeeze. "They won't find us."

But the calm cracks. We head back, scanning the sky.

The afternoon passes in contingency planning—new drone patrol patterns, remote noise generators to confuse thermal scans. By dusk, we're mentally fried. Anderssen volunteers to grill salmon on the deck. Rae whips up lemon-dill couscous and charred asparagus.

At the long cedar table, with floor-to-ceiling windows reopened to the valley twilight, dinner feels almost like a vacation. Conversation drifts to normal things: Anderssen's hobby forging knives, Rae's attempt to brew kombucha that exploded. Cam tells a story about painting a community mural in Rio that locals protected with lawn chairs and nightly karaoke.

Laughter stirs the air, and my stress loosens. I study Cam's face in candlelight—how the glow warms her freckle constellation, how grief at last night's terror moves to the background. Hope flickers.

After dessert (Rae's canned peaches flambéed with bourbon), Anderssen and Rae excuse themselves. Anderssen to the perimeter, Rae to the command station. Cam and I linger, flames in the hearth crackling behind us.

Sawyer

She runs a fingertip around the rim of her wine glass. "Would it break discipline if I challenged you to a rematch from this morning? No mats."

"What do you have in mind?"

She pushes back her chair, stands, and offers her hand. "Bedroom floor."

Blood surges. I rise, link our fingers, and lead her down the dim hallway. With every step the air thickens—anticipation and the lingering scent of woodsmoke. We pass the secured Faraday office, the silent gallery of blank canvases waiting for safer days. At the master suite entrance she stops me, and palms my chest.

"I need tonight to erase that ticking, Sawyer." Her voice shakes with honesty. "Erase the picture of you kneeling before that bomb."

I brush my lips over her forehead. "Then let's paint something louder."

We barely cross the threshold before our hands roam. Her mouth finds mine, eager, tasting of bourbon peaches. I cup her jaw, angle for deeper, our tongues sliding together in a slow promise. She pushes up my Henley, her soft fingertips grazing my bare skin. I shiver, discarding the shirt. Her top follows—soft cotton drawn over her head, revealing a pale blue lace bralette.

"Color's nearly matching the lake," I murmur, tracing the lace edge.

"Wait until you see the set." She smirks, stepping back to shimmy out of her leggings, leaving a matching lace thong. I drink her in—sun-kissed curves, and strength from this morning's training.

"You are lethal," I whisper. I approach, trapping her between me and the wall. Our bodies align, and heat leaps. She drags her nails lightly down my spine, eliciting a rumble from my chest.

I pepper kisses along her neck, over her collarbone, and down the slope of each breast restrained by lace. Her breaths hitch into tiny gasps. I slip a hand behind her back, unclasp her bra, and let the fabric drop. The sight steals the air from my lungs. I lower my mouth, and worship her. Gentle, then greedy. She tugs my hair, whispering my name like a prayer.

We move toward the bed but stumble, laughing, and land on the plush rug instead. I lay her down, moonlight silvering her skin through the skylight. She looks up—eyes dark, trusting, blazing.

"Your turn," she says, tugging at my pants' waistband. I strip away my pants and briefs, the remaining barrier. Her gaze rakes eagerly, then softens. "Beautiful," she whispers, palming my cock. It hardens instantly from her touch.

"You're the one who is beautiful."

Kissing her again is like coming home to a storm you crave. Our hands explore familiar terrain made new by hunger. Her thigh hooks around my waist, and I drag my fingers up her calf, savoring all of her.

"Ready?" I murmur against her lips.

She rolls her hips in answer, desperate. "Now."

I guide her thighs, position, then enter her with a slow slide. We gasp together, our passion igniting. I hold still, letting her adjust. "Fuck, this is…" my words fall away.

She presses her forehead to mine, finishing my thought, "Perfect."

With that, my self-control unravels.

We find a rhythm, slow deep strokes that savor rather than rush. Each thrust pushes soft sounds from her throat. Her hands roam my back, her nails leaving trails. I kiss along her jaw, her ear. She arches, murmuring encouragement—"more, Sawyer, please."

Heat coils tight. I change the angle, hitting a spot that makes her cry out. She shatters first, body trembling, pulling me deeper. Seeing her unravel triggers my own release.

I groan her name, riding waves of pleasure that blur edges of reality.

After, we remain tangled on the rug, hearts drumming. I stroke her hair from her damp forehead as she traces lazy circles on my chest.

"No bombs, no reporters," she whispers. "Just us."

I kiss her temple. "World can burn. We'll paint it back brighter."

She smiles sleepily. "Promise?"

"On every brush you own."

When we finally crawl into bed, exhaustion tugs but peace settles deeper. She sprawls across my chest as I adjust the duvet, then key the bedside panel to arm the night sensors.

Because here, on this mountain, behind encrypted doors, our line is more than lasers and steel. It's skin to skin, heartbeat to heartbeat—until the outside world recedes into hush and only our breaths map the future.

18

Camille

Nothing smells like new beginnings the way fresh paint does—oily, mineral, a hush of possibility hovering the second the cap twists off. The great room at Bastion is our studio today: tarps taped to slate slabs, windows thrown open so pine air spins inside and mixes with the scent of turpentine. Early light pours down the A-frame ceiling, and Sawyer stands at my side, sleeves rolled, expression equal parts curiosity and latent battle readiness.

"I'm trusting you not to mock my inner Picasso," he warns, eyeing the blank canvas perched on an easel we hauled from the supplies closet.

"I would never," I say, dipping a flat brush into cerulean. "But be aware I own photographic evidence of your first attempt."

"Blackmail material," he grumbles, but a smile tugs at his mouth.

I hand him a palette already dabbed with cobalt, burnt umber, titanium white. "Lesson one: paint speaks faster than words. Don't overthink. Lay color, then decide what it's trying to say."

His brow furrows. "That sounds… spiritual."

"It is." I guide his fingers around the brush handle, our skin touching, sparks flaring up my arm. "Like your bomb work—muscle memory plus instinct. The only consequence here is ugly wall art."

He exhales, raises the brush, and—after a glance at me for permission—drags a wide swipe of cerulean across the canvas. The stroke is hesitant, straight as a laser. I laugh softly.

"You paint like you're drawing a security perimeter," I tease.

He huffs. "Occupational hazard."

I lift my own brush, slash a diagonal streak of raw sienna right through his blue—a reckless, messy Z. "There. Now soften the edge."

He tilts his head. "How?"

I step behind him, pressing my chest to his back, guiding his hand with mine. Together we feather the wet edge, blue and brown bleeding into smoky twilight. His breath catches as my heart trills. The sensation of his muscles flexing under my palms is dangerously distracting.

"See?" I whisper. "Art is a conversation. Even the interruptions become the point."

"Conversation. Copy that." He breaks free, dips into ochre, dots small bursts across the haze. "Stars?"

"Or tracer rounds," I joke, but his grin says he'll allow the poetic version tonight.

For an hour we trade strokes—some bold, some timid. He loosens, shoulders dropping, lines turning fluid. He smears a swath of midnight purple as I carve a river of viridian through it. Together, we splash raincloud gray with a toothbrush flick, and then he risks a finger-paint swirl, spreading white and gold into galaxies. And somewhere between color choices and shared laughs, the undercurrent between us swells like a rising tide.

"Your turn," he says finally, stepping back to examine the riot of abstraction. He's streaked with crimson on his jaw, a smear of teal on his forearm. My personal masterpiece. He eyes my untouched skin, then dips his thumb into cadmium red and swipes it gently across my collarbone, just above the neckline of my tank.

"Marking territory?" I challenge.

"Creating dialogue," he answers, his voice low and steady.

The air thickens. I set my brush in the turp jar, wiping my hands on a rag, and then walk toward him, my hips thrumming. "We could blend more layers," I suggest, feather-light fingertip tracing the crimson on his jaw.

"We could," he murmurs, snagging my paint-stained hand, lifting it to his mouth. He kisses the inside of my wrist—soft, deliberate. Heat rolls through me.

I step closer until my paint-splattered chest brushes his. "I've always wanted a live canvas," I whisper. "Think you can hold still?"

A spark leaps in his eyes. Pure hunger. "Try me."

He peels off his fitted white T-shirt, exposing his weapon-forged physique scarred with muted memories. I dip a clean brush into ultramarine and, with exaggerated care, paint a winding line from his left shoulder down across his sternum. He holds steady, gaze riveted to my lips. I swirl the line, add copper arcs mimicking topographic maps. When I reach his abdomen he inhales sharply.

"Ticklish?" I tease.

"Anticipating."

I tilt the brush handle, draw it lower, just skimming the V of his hip. His breath hitches as mine echoes. Craving sparks along every nerve. I set the brush aside, and with my fingers, I smear the paint—blue and copper mixing, my hands exploring. His skin is warm and alive.

Sawyer

He reaches for me, tugging my tank over my head, tossing it aside. The mountain air skates over my paint-dappled skin, but his heated gaze scorches. I back him carefully until his shoulders meet the wall beside the windows, then press both hands to his chest and lean in, trailing open-mouthed kisses across paint and scars. He groans, tilts his head back, surrendering.

I lick a path from his jaw to his collarbone. "Still holding still?"

"Barely."

"Good." I drag my teeth across his pectoral as his hands tangle in my hair. He lifts me by the waist, barefoot feet dangling for an instant before my back meets the unfinished canvas behind us. Wet paint squishes cool against my shoulder blades, contrasting the molten ache building everywhere else. I gasp.

"Now you're art," he growls, capturing my mouth. The kiss is slow only for a heartbeat, and then hunger takes over. His tongue strokes deep, commanding. I meet it with matching fervor. Paint smears between us, the colors blending across our skin.

His hands slide down, and hook under my thighs. Instinctively, I lock my legs around his hips. Even through denim his hardness presses where I ache most. Desire flares white-hot. He boosts me higher, lips leaving mine to skim the sensitive underside of my jaw, nipping gently.

I clutch his shoulders. "Sawyer—"

He meets my eyes, breathing harsh. "I want you in every shade."

"Then take me," I whisper.

In answer, he carries me—still wrapped around him—across the room to the long reclaimed-wood table we used for mixing palettes. With a sweep of his forearm he clears brushes and jars, scattering them in a clatter along the drop cloth. I feel a guilty pang for the mess but the heat between us obliterates everything. He sets me atop the cool wood, and I recline, my hair spilling over the edge.

He peels my sports bra away, sucking a nipple into his mouth. I arch, a moan ripping out. His tongue is hot, perfect. His hand glides down my stomach, fingers hooking the waistband of my shorts. He meets my gaze, a silent permission. I nod. In a fluid motion he slides my shorts and panties off, and drops them to the floor.

Cool air kisses my flushed skin; but his warm palm parts my thighs, kneels slightly, and drags just the pad of his thumb over my slickness. I shiver, clutching the edge of the table.

"Beautiful," he murmurs, dipping inside just enough to tease. I writhe.

I tug his belt, fumbling the buckle. He offers help, pushing his jeans down, releasing his dick. I glide my palm along him.

"I need you" he says, his voice pure gravel.

"I need you more," I pant. He fists his cock with one hand, and then he strokes his hands up my calves to my knees, lifting my legs over his shoulders like I'm weightless. The stretch is exquisite. He positions, pauses—eyes locked to mine.

"You're mine," he rasps.

"Yes, all yours."

He thrusts slow but deep as my breath catches, stars scatter behind my closed lids. He stills, letting me adjust, then withdraws, sliding back in with greater force. Pleasure spirals hot. The table creaks.

Our pace finds a rhythm—urgent yet drawn-out, each roll measured so every nerve registers. My legs slide from his shoulders, and wrap around his waist for leverage, meeting each thrust. He groans my name like a confession.

Pressure builds, coils, luminous. His thumb circles where I need him most. My hips jerk. I teeter on the brink, and he thrusts harder—once, twice—and I tumble over, gasping his name, every muscle clenching tight. He follows with a guttural exhale, riding the wave, spilling into a praise-laced murmur against my ear.

We collapse together, sticky with sweat and paint, lungs heaving. He peppers kisses along my hairline, whispering, "You okay?"

"Beyond." My laugh is shaky joy. "We ruined the table."

He glances at cobalt fingerprints dotting the plank. "Battle scars." He lifts his crimson-blue-smeared hand, studies it like a masterpiece. Then slides a fingertip across my cheek, leaving a streak. "Yours now."

I cup the back of his neck, and pull him into a soft, lingering kiss tasting of satisfaction and promise. Outside the windows the last of dusk bleeds pink over distant peaks, humanity nowhere else in sight.

Later we'll wipe the floors, decode new police intel, and plan a strategy. But right now the only strategy is entwining limbs, curling on the paint-spattered rug, and drifting into drowsy contentment while the wind sighs through pines and the world holds its breath just for us.

If this is what normal can look like—brushstrokes, breathless laughter, skin against skin—then I'll fight gallery openings, bomb scares, and jealous tabloids for it. I'll paint a thousand walls until they mirror the sky Sawyer just carved across my canvas skin.

And he? He'll stand guard not just with weapons but with overwhelming love that feels as indelible as the stains now swirling purple on our chests.

19

Sawyer

The safe-house feels different now that we're packing to leave—like it's exhaling after holding its breath for forty-eight straight hours. Every plank and beam still hums with the memory of color-splashed kisses and skin-on-skin confessions, but practicalities elbow romance aside as flight cases and gun bags clutter the foyer.

I crouch beside a pelican case, securing the foam cradle that keeps our encrypted laptops from jostling. My mind drifts backward: Cam's laughter echoing through the A-frame, the neon-blue streak she left on my ribs, slow mornings tangled in linen while fog rose out of the pines. Forty-eight hours off-grid and I've tasted a life I didn't realize I craved. Now I have to shove us both back into the chessboard where someone's still trying to knock her off the squares.

Footsteps crunch on gravel outside. Anderssen's voice booms: "Fuel topped, convoy green." Rae chimes through comms inside, "Perimeter drones docking." The house is orchestrating its own goodbye.

Cam appears at the top of the stairs with an armful of supplies—sketchbooks, a quart jar of brushes, tubes rubber-banded in a bouquet. She wears jean shorts, hiking boots, and my black BRAVO hoodie four sizes too big, sleeves shoved past paint-speckled elbows. A sadness flickers behind her smile.

"This place was starting to feel like a studio retreat," she says, descending. "Back to reality."

"Kingsley House won't know what hit it," I answer, closing the case. "Paint stains on every imported rug."

"Gregory will faint." She tries for levity but it lands shallow. She drops her supplies into a tote, then runs a thumb along a fresh bruise on her thigh—proof of yesterday's "lesson" on disarming a wrist-grab that turned into something else entirely. A flush rises on her cheeks at the memory.

I slip closer, and hook a finger under her chin. "You okay?"

She eyes the door, voice low. "What if we go back and the note … or worse … happens again?"

"It might," I admit, because false comfort is toxic. "But I'll catch them."

She searches my face. "And if I'm the bait again?"

"Then I'll be the trap. We drew them out once. We'll finish it." I stroke her jaw. "Walls and doors, remember?"

Her shoulders lower. She nods, leaning into a quick kiss that tastes of anxiety trimmed with trust.

Anderssen barges in, lugging a crate of shotgun shells. "Birds are singing, coffee's brewed, and our prints are wiped. Let's bounce before paparazzi sniff the ridge."

"Kingsley House is buttoned?" I ask.

He sets the crate down. "Dean flew in a private security contractor to harden Level-I glass on every ground-floor pane. Extra K-9s sweep the exterior hourly. Hartley's undercover unit will tail the perimeter for seventy-two hours. If the mole twitches, we'll know."

That's the official line; it still tastes like thin soup. I holster my SIG, grip Anderssen on the shoulder. "Good work, brother."

"Just keep your head clear." His gaze flicks to Cam.

"Got it."

My phone buzzes. It's Dean's satellite line. I accept. "Status?"

"Kingsley House is operational and paparazzi diverted. PD scrubbed staff comms; one caterer texted a tabloid cousin about the bomb but no direct link to the perp. Keep eyes peeled for inside cameras tampered before the gala."

"Copy. We're wheels up in twenty."

He pauses. "Sawyer, remember: protect the principal, collect evidence, but don't escalate without probable cause."

"I know the drill." But my tone is pure flint. Dean catches it.

"And keep your heart out of the trigger guard."

Too late.

WE SNAKE DOWN THE MOUNTAIN. The lead SUV is driven by Anderssen, mine in the middle with Cam beside me, and Rae bringing up the rear. Cam's earbuds play a lo-fi playlist but she pulls one bud out every five minutes to ask: "Can you really track a drone feed in motion?" "Will paparazzi still be there?" "What's first thing you'll do when this is over?" I answer each patiently. ("Yes," "Probably," "Kiss you in public.") That last one steals her breath—and mine.

A news notification beeps on her phone. Instinctively, she silences it but the glare says the headline was ugly. "Maybe it'll blow over now that we left," she mutters.

"It will blow over when I string their ringleader up in court." I flick the turn signal at a switchback. "I still lean inside job. Last night Rae found a data logger on a defunct access point at Kingsley House—someone piggybacked internal Wi-Fi to send those gala photos."

Her mouth tightens. "Someone I grew up seeing every day?" The betrayal laces her voice.

"Or a temp contractor. The search narrows." I brush her thigh, trying my best to comfort her. She covers my hand and squeezes.

The mansion looks unchanged when we reach it. From the outside you'd never tell of all the changes. But up close, new bullet-resistant glass is noticeable, a faint green sheen across the lower windows. Two black K-9 SUVs idle; officers walk shepherds along the hedges. There's a paparazzi camp beyond the gates, their lenses like gun barrels. They surge when our convoy rolls in.

Cam stiffens. I park beneath the porte cochère. Immediately Riggs and Anderssen form a shield, Rae coordinating luggage.

Gregory strides out, relief etched deep. "Pumpkin!" He engulfs Cam before she unbuckles.

Inside the foyer, the smell of new varnish mixes with lily arrangements leftover from the gala. Gregory pulls me aside into the study lined with leather-bound volumes.

"Thank you," he says, closing the door. "House feels like a fortress. Still, Cam mentioned you think it's an inside leak?"

"Yes. Gala photo came from our own network. I'll interview each contractor personally." I slide a folder onto his desk—names, background flags. "I also urge you to suspend deliveries and limit staff rotations."

He rubs his temples. "Our chefs quit on the spot after the bomb fiasco. Replacements start tomorrow."

"That's a vulnerability," I warn. "No one new until we vet them."

He hesitates. Investor brunch is in three days. But he nods. "Do it."

We exit. Cam waits by the stairwell, hugging her tote of brushes like a life raft. I cross, lowering my voice. "Why don't you finish the lake scene in your studio? I'll sweep the east wing."

She catches my arm. "Stay close?"

"Always." I squeeze, then gesture Rae to shadow her upstairs.

⸻

INTERVIEWING the staff would normally fall to Anderssen or Rae, but I want to look each suspect in the eye.

I interrogate the Kingsley gardener (alibi: hospitalized mother), the IT subcontractor (cleared via MAC log), a new maid recommended by an agency (nervous but clean). By 18:10 Anderssen reports no anomalies.

But my gut churns. Something still rots. I join Riggs in the security room—twelve monitors feed from new cameras. He rewinds gala footage again. We freeze on an image of the catering corridor camera at 22:18—just before the bomb. A figure in chef whites pushes a trash bin. The badge ID tag blurs.

I zoom. Riggs curses. "Badge is a photocopy."

"Cross-check photo with agency files," I bark. Anderssen inputs—no match. So the bomber was inside that night disguised as waitstaff. Access given by the replaced catering team.

My phone vibrates. It's Cam.

Dinner break? I made sandwiches. Olive loaf—don't judge. Veranda.

I smile despite the gloom and head toward the veranda.

The house is quieter. Gregory's in his office, and the staff is minimal. Cam sets two plates on a small round table overlooking the garden. The sandwiches are crooked, mustard heavy. I bite anyway, and it tastes like normal life.

She eyes monitors visible through the archway. "Find anything?"

"Suspect used a fake badge, and borrowed a uniform." I push lettuce aside. "We'll track them."

Her shoulders slump. "I'll never feel safe again, will I?"

I lean, brushing my knuckles across her cheek. "You will. Safety isn't the absence of threats; it's the presence of trust. In me. In yourself."

She blinks tears away. "I trust you. But what happens when this is over? Do you return to defusing bombs elsewhere?"

"I return to wherever you hang your canvases." The truth clears a fog I didn't know I still carried. "The job might end, but I'm not stepping out of your frame."

She exhales shakily—half laugh, half sob—then kisses me, mustard and all. Heat ignites, but I keep it tempered because the hall cameras still run.

"Careful," I murmur, pulling back. "I still have interviews."

"Tonight?" She pouts.

"Duty, then bedtime. I promise."

She pins a paint-smeared sticky note on my chest: **"Trust your gut."** Then she heads upstairs.

I tuck the note in my pocket.

The rest of the day passes in a blur. Duty done. Suspect list trimmed to three: a food-runner who vanished after his shift, a florist assistant with fake references, and the recently fired COO Spencer DeLuca (no alibi, known grudge).

Cam opens her door at my soft knock. She's in a cotton nightdress, hair down. Her smile is both exhaustion and relief.

"Hall post or inside?" she teases.

"Inside," I say, stepping in, bolting the door. "I kept my promise."

She slips her hand under my shirt, over my abdomen, eyes shining. "I painted after dinner—found a new shade of lake blue."

"I'd like to see," I whisper, nuzzling her neck.

"Tomorrow," she answers, mouth finding mine. "Tonight, let's make our own color."

We do.

Between breaths she whispers fear, hope, unspoken vows. Between kisses I assure, vow, plan. Outside, threats still lurk, but inside the echo of her laughter against my skin, they lose shape.

And tomorrow, when dawn floods the windows, I'll track that food-runner's rental car, dig through florist invoices, and corner DeLuca's last known associate—because safety is more than walls and doors. It's finishing the battle so she never has to look over her shoulder again.

Until then, I hold her—steady, fierce—while the storm outside hunts for cracks it will never find.

20

Camille

I'm mixing lake blues again—three parts ultramarine, one part phthalo, a breath of Payne's gray—when my phone buzzes face-down on the studio table. I ignore it at first. The morning light slants across my canvas, turning the wet paint into a slab of water I can almost step into, and I don't want to be tugged back to reality where reporters hunch outside our gates and my life is an itinerary of camera angles and safe words.

The phone buzzes again. And again.

I wipe my fingers on a rag and flip it over.

Dad.

Dad: Pumpkin, come meet me in the garden for tea. I miss you.

I scan the studio's corners—windows latched, door ajar to the corridor where Rae's footsteps just passed five minutes ago. I can still smell Sawyer's cedar-and-wool ghost from when he popped in earlier to kiss my hair and promise he'd be two rooms away in the security den.

I type back *On my way*, then hesitate. Protocol whispers: *Text Sawyer.* Pride answers: *It'll be sixty seconds.* My thumb hovers over his name. A second message arrives before I decide.

Come alone. Quick.

That prickle climbs my spine, the one my body learned somewhere between the first threat letter and the bomb. It's ridiculous—It's dad. And yet…

I grab my phone, my small pocket pepper spray, the slim palette knife I've used as a box opener, and slip into the hall. "Be right back," I call toward no one, hoping Rae hears it through the open command room door. Stupid. I know better. But the south garden gate has always been the least formal place to talk— delivery drivers, dog walkers, Gregory's spontaneous meetings.

The house is quiet as a museum. The blue runners swallow my barefoot pads. At the conservatory, the air shifts— cooler, fragrant with damp soil and crushed geranium leaf. I push through the glass door to the terrace. Sunshine hits me like a cymbal crash.

Beyond the rose arbor, the south lawn unspools in clipped emerald, dotted with white garden chairs we never remember to bring inside. The breeze carries a thread of diesel, faint and wrong among jasmine.

The service drive.

"Hello?" I call, rounding the hedge toward the wrought-iron side gate.

A white panel van idles nose-in at the curb cut, unmarked except for a magnetic orange hazard triangle slapped haphazardly on the back. The garden service sometimes uses rentals when a truck goes into the shop. Normal. It's normal. The driver's side door stands open, no one visible.

I step closer, heart rate flicking upward like a metronome cranked too fast. "Hey? Have you seen my father?"

The van's sliding door snaps open so fast the sound knifes through the air. Two figures burst out—coveralls, caps, masks that aren't masks so much as cheap PPE—the kind everyone wore in 2020. One grabs my elbow, the other my waist.

Every nerve I honed in the safe house lights up.

Wrist rotate, heel stomp, knee.

I twist toward the thumb, wrench free, slam my heel onto the instep of the one on my right. He swears, grip loosening. I drive my knee toward the other's groin with everything Sawyer drilled into me.

Sawyer

"Get off me!" I shout, lungs ripping. It's an ugly, desperate sound, not the polished charity-gala version of me, and I don't care. "Help—!"

A hand clamps over my mouth. The chemical tang of nitrile gloves and something like solvent fills my nose, stinging. The heavier one bears down, shoving me toward the grass. I pitch sideways on instinct. I twist and bite. My teeth meet rubber. He yelps. I use the moment to jam my thumb into the soft corner of his eye socket. His head snaps back.

I try to sprint.

The third shape materializes from behind the hedge. I didn't even see him exit the driver's seat. He takes me at the knees—tackle perfect enough to make a football coach weep—and I hit the lawn with a breathless *whuff*. The sky fractures—blue, hedge, van, blue—as the world spins. My phone flies out, cartwheels across the grass, and skids under the van. I lunge, and a hand wrenches my wrist back hard enough to send lightning up my arm.

"Stop fighting," a voice snarls, low through fabric. "Don't make me break it."

They flip me. Grass blades stick to my cheek. Chlorophyll and panic flood my mouth.

"Help!" I scream into the glove. The word dies against latex. "Saw—"

Another palm smothers the sound.

They haul me upright. The heavier one yanks my arms behind me, plastic biting—zip tie ratcheting down too fast. My watch digs into bone. I thrash. From somewhere far away, a dog barks. Closer, the fountain keeps burbling.

The third guy slaps a strip of tape across my mouth. Silver—industrial, stale adhesive reeking of dust and glue. My stomach flips.

I kick—wild and ugly. My bare foot connects with a shin. A hiss, a curse. Hands tighten in retaliation.

"Move," the driver says. The syllables are so ordinary they terrify me more than a growl would have.

They half-drag, half-carry me to the van. My heel clips the lip of the step. Pain explodes up my calf. My eyes water, and the world blurs. I register details because that's all I have left: a scratch beside the handle, paint worn to primer; a sticker inside the door—*Maintain proper load distribution*. As if this were about cargo.

They shove me inside. The metal floor is ridged and cold under my thighs. The air reeks of oil, old coffee, something chemical like bleach half-rinsed from mops. There are no seats, just tie-down loops and a few plastic crates bungeed to the wall.

I squirm to my knees, aiming for the far door. Someone's forearm slams across my back, pinning me. The sliding

Sawyer

door whispers shut. Darkness swallows light like a wave crashing.

The engine deepens. We lurch, tires thumping over uneven pavers, then smooth out as we hit asphalt.

No.

No.

I slam my head back into whoever's bracing me. My skull connects with a chin. Another curse. I scoot sideways, trying to wedge my shoulder into a seam to lever up, to do *something*. One of them grabs my ankle and yanks. The world tilts, and I sprawl. A knee presses into my hip, hard enough to bruise.

I force my jaw to work against tape, feeling the sticky edges lift and reseal and lift with every ragged breath. My tongue tastes like glue. I picture Sawyer's hands, the careful way he freed me from zip ties when we practiced, the way he said *you don't have to win; you just have to break the script*. I will not give them compliance. I will announce a mess.

I roll my wrist as far as the zip will allow, hunting for the small metal nub on my smartwatch—panic function. Sawyer made me promise to wear it. Triple-click, hold.

I mash. Once. Twice. Three times. The haptic motor flutters against my skin like a trapped moth. No tone—silent mode—but there's a *feel* to it, a stuttering like a heartbeat. Please. Send. Please.

The van accelerates. Through the thin metal I feel the change in road surface. The soft-thud rhythm of expansion joints says we've hit a major boulevard. A second later, a higher whine—freeway merge.

The driver mutters something I can't catch over the engine. The others shift as they settle in. My captor's knee eases off my hip a fraction. I let my body go limp, counting silently. Thirty heartbeats. Forty. The tempo of tires changes; we hit a patch of rougher pavement, then smooth again. A faint curve presses my shoulder against a wheel well— banking right. The air tastes drier, dustier. Not the moist breath of the bay. Inland? Or am I inventing that to feel less helpless?

My cheek is mashed to the rubber mat. Every vibration rattles my jaw. Tears leak sideways into my ear. I bite them back. I'm not crying for them. I'm crying because this body I've been trying to love is now cargo.

I inch my chin, trying to scrape the tape on the ribbed floor. The adhesive peels a millimeter before smearing back down. I freeze when one of them shifts, then try again. Peel. Press. Peel. The tape stretches invisibly. My skin stings.

A hand fists in my hair, yanking my head up so much the pain stars me. "We can make this easy," he says through the mask. "Or we can make it loud."

Sawyer

Make it loud, Sawyer said once about defiance. I stare at the eyes above the mask—pale, the lashes gloved with sweat. I can't speak. But I can stare. I make my gaze ice.

He lets go with a shove. My scalp screams.

I shift my shoulders and feel the slim ridge of my palette knife under my tank, tucked into the waistband where I shoved it without thinking. God. Hope is a blade with dull teeth. I wedge my wrists against my spine, fishing for it with the tips of my numb fingers. The zip tie eats skin every time I flex. I find the knife's handle with my pinky, but the angle is wrong; my fingers won't close. I try to roll, to change the geometry. Someone's boot thumps my ribs—warning, not full force, but enough to tell me they'll escalate if I keep wriggling.

I stop. Breathe through my nose. We exit—downshift rumble, a hollow slap as tires cross a raised seam—then a left, immediate right. I try to build a map in my head. It unspools like a bad drawing, lines looping in the wrong places. Panic eats at the corners of it, nibbling. I shove it back. One line at a time.

When I close my eyes I see Sawyer in the hallway feed, calm in a storm, hands steady on a ticking thing that wanted to erase us. I imagine him now, radio crackling, eyes going to the south camera feed when Rae says the word *ping* in that tightly contained voice she gets. I imagine him running. It helps and hurts, both.

They talk over me like I'm a package. "Fifteen out." "Traffic's clear." "The device?" "Stashed." Words drop like pebbles into a lake, leaving ripples of meaning I can't fully catch.

My arms burn. My jaw aches. A sob tries to elbow up my throat. I choke it down with bile and glue. My mind starts doing awful arithmetic again: what I didn't say to Vanessa this morning because I was in a rush; the shade of blue I'll never finish if I don't get back; the portrait of my mother I started when I was fourteen and abandoned because the line of her mouth made me cry.

I force my brain to think of stupid things. The hum of the tires modulates like a wrong-key lullaby. The floor smells like nine hundred coffee deliveries and three broken bottles of cleaner. There's grit pressed into my cheek. I lick it from the tape edge with the tip of my tongue; it tastes like salt and dirt and the inside of a toolbox.

Time gets liquid. It stretches, snaps back, stretches again. At some point the van slows. The brakes squeal in a way rental fleets never fix. We turn—left, I think—and roll onto gravel. The van rocks. The engine idles, then cuts.

Silence lands so hard I think I've gone deaf. Then a door bangs open and heat roars in where the cold had been, dry and baked. The doors slide. The world glares white. I squint.

"Out," someone says.

Sawyer

Hands hook my elbows. I plant my feet and make my body the heaviest thing I can. It doesn't matter; they've done this before; they swing and I stumble, knees catching, skin tearing on grit. They yank me upright again. The horizon is a smear past the rectangle of brightness. It could be anywhere—industrial yard, back road, storage facility. A white wall looms, blind and featureless.

I crane my neck, searching for the sky. It's a hard cobalt with heat pulsing off it in waves. Somewhere a plane needles its way across, a tin speck. I want to scream up at it that I'm here, I'm still here, find me.

A hand shoves between my shoulders. I go forward into shadow—another interior, cooler, stale with the ghost of solvents and dust.

As the door clangs shut behind us, a single thought knifes cleanly through the noise.

Make it loud.

I inhale as deep as the tape allows, then slam my heel down and back with every ounce of rage in me. I don't feel contact; I *hear* it—the ugly thunk of heel to shin, a grunt. A hand whips across my cheek, knocking my head sideways, bright spots popping. Pain blooms. I stagger. They shove, and I trip. The floor rises, and the world tilts.

In the flash before I hit, I picture Sawyer's gray eyes, savage soft, the way they looked when he said *after*. I picture the little white line he painted on my canvas, the shield hidden under chaos, and I glue myself to that memory the way the tape glues my mouth, the way the zip tie glues my hands.

I hit the ground.

I don't break.

I don't give.

I don't stop counting turns. I don't stop cataloging sounds. I don't stop being the wall and the door in my own small, bound, shaking way. I force breath in and out through my nose, slow and controlled.

Because he is coming. Because I am not a package. Because color is louder than blood. Because the story isn't done.

And because someone, somewhere, is going to regret underestimating an artist with paint under her nails and a soldier in her heart.

21

Sawyer

The alert hits like a fist to the throat.

Rae's voice cracks over comms from the command room: "Trip-click SOS from Cam's watch. South garden cam just went to snow. I'm rolling back ten seconds—three shadows—white panel van. Blind spot… *fuck*."

I'm already moving. The tablet on my desk clatters to the floor as I bolt out of the security den, sprinting past the conservatory into hard noon light. My earpiece hums with overlapping voices—Riggs barking for gate freeze, Anderssen pivoting K-9 to the south hedge, Rae dumping coordinates to SPPD—but all I hear is the echo of Cam's laugh this morning and the fact that I am not where I promised I would be.

The south lawn is a smear of emerald and sunlight. The fountain burbles obscenely calm. Beyond the rose arbor, tire dust hangs in the air in a thin, shimmering ribbon. In the service cutout at the curb, faint rubber crescents mark where a van scrubbed hard, reversed, and punched it.

I inhale, and taste diesel.

"White panel, no markings," Anderssen's voice clips. "Gate six shows outflow. LPR didn't pop—plate covered."

"Check the overflow cam," I rasp, dropping to my knees in the grass. There—by the hedge—two inches of plastic like shark skin, a torn tail of a black zip tie. A silver smear on a blade of grass—duct tape adhesive. A phone case face-down under the lip of the drive—hers. Rage detonates.

"Code Black," I say flat. "Internal lockdown. Push out BOLO to SPPD: White panel van, 2014 to 2017 body style, high roof. Three male suspects. Last seen south exit, eastbound."

Rae: "Copy. Dispatch notified. Watch ping got one location before it went dark—jammer kicked in. Last hit is on Dutton near the 115 on-ramp. I'm scraping SP-trans cams."

Riggs thunders up, breath hard, eyes harder. "Where?"

I point to the grass. He sees what I see—the scuff marks, the heel divot where she fought. He picks up the zip tail, palms the tape scrap with gloved fingers, and bags them fast. "She fought 'em," he says, like a prayer that doubles as a war cry.

I force my lungs to steady. "Rae, pull the south garden feed for twenty minutes prior. Did we get a face at any approach?"

"Negative—someone blasted it with a narrowband jammer and angled the lens with a hook from the blind spot. They knew the grid."

"Inside help," Riggs growls.

"Yeah." My jaw grinds. We were hunting a mole, and the mole just bared its teeth.

I scan the hedges, the service lane, the angle of sunlight, making a mental model I can walk backward in my mind. I taste metal. I pocket the phone case, and stand. "Rae, pull every van rental contract within a three-mile radius from this morning. Anderssen, expand perimeter—check drains, alleys for dropped items. Hartley's unit?"

"Rolling," Rae says. "ETA four."

"Launch the drone," I say, already running back into the house. "Vector down Dutton and 115—we'll lose altitude near the freeway, but give me what you can."

"Bird up in sixty seconds."

12:12 — Command room is ice-cold and humming. I slam the door, yank the Faraday cage panel closed behind me—

no phones, no bleed. Rae's up on four monitors, fingers flying. A dot blinks—Cam's last watch ping—then dies. A second screen fills with SP-trans feeds: blurs of concrete and steel, streaks of light on asphalt.

"There," Rae says, stabbing a frame—an overhead lane camera catching the tail of a white van ducking behind a box truck near the on-ramp. Plate smeared with mud or covered. "No hazard triangle visible. Could be it, could be any of twenty lookalikes."

"Angle me a reflection," I mutter. "Pull the windshield glare from the truck's chrome."

Rae grins—teeth bared. "Now we're cooking." She magnifies a six-by-six patch of glare, inverts, filters. The universe cooperates: a spectral smear resolves into the faintest ghost of a van profile with a dent low on the passenger door and a sticker—tiny orange triangle—half peeled. "Gotcha," she whispers.

I key my throat mic. "All teams, this is One. We have a unique—orange hazard triangle on the back door, passenger-side dent knee-height. Notify CHP. Priority. Van took 115 south. Last ping minute twelve."

Riggs: "I'll swing south on the causeway. Anderssen keeps the house tight."

"Negative," I snap. "We don't split. We feed the net and we hunt the leak."

Sawyer

Silence. Then: "Copy," Riggs says with a clipped tone.

My tablet hums with incoming: CHP acknowledges, BOLO broadcast to patrol units along 115. Hartley chimes in: "We're on the freeway now. Tell me if your drone gets eyes."

"Bird is overhead—altitude down to legal. We've got twenty white vans. Filtering."

Out of the corner of my vision, a little pink sticky note flutters on the edge of the console—the one she pinned to my chest last night: *Trust your gut.* My hand shakes once as I anchor it on the desk.

"Dean?" I say, stabbing the satphone.

He picks up in a breath. "Talk."

"Cam's grabbed. White panel van, three male perps, inside assist probable. They jammed our cam and sprinted south. Last ping at the 115 on-ramp."

Dead air. Then: "We're spinning up. Orange-Plus Team is in the air in thirty. You're lead, Sawyer. Don't do anything stupid alone."

I stare at the monitors, at the emptiness that is a screen without the person you love on it, and feel something in me go diamond hard. "No promises."

The house turns into a hive. PD locks lanes near the on-ramp as they chase phantom vans. Drone hops feed towers, catches pieces. Every piece mocks me. Cam's last breadcrumb is that ping and the way the grass bent where she fought. She fought—that helps—but every passing minute is a mile of road.

We tear the inside of Kingsley House apart with a polite smile. Rae traces the text that pinged Cam to the garden. "Spoofed," she says, frowning. "Sender masked under a known contact, rerouted through a bot farm. Whoever did this borrowed trust to open the door."

"Inside," I grind. "They knew the number to fake that would get her moving."

Who? A friend? A staff member?

I need to move or I'll put my fist through a screen. I stride into the hall, intending to sweep contractor comms for the fifth time, and almost plow into Gregory Kingsley.

He looks ten years older than this morning. His tie is loosened; one shirt sleeve is rolled, the other still buttoned; his hair is finger-combed, not perfect. He's carrying a glass he probably meant to drink but hasn't. He lifts his head at me, and the relief I want to see doesn't arrive. Something else does: dread, then guilt, then the kind of iron I only saw in platoon leaders right before they confessed to ordering a thing that went sideways.

"Mr. Kingsley," I say, keeping my voice neutral.

"Come," he says, hoarse. "My office."

Sawyer

I follow, shutting the door. He stands at the window overlooking the drive where press vans have clustered like vultures and swat aside my urge to rip them in half.

He doesn't turn when he speaks. "I never wanted her hurt."

It's such a non sequitur that for a heartbeat I miss it. Then my blood runs cold.

"Explain," I say. Not a question.

He doesn't immediately. He taps the glass with one knuckle, watching the distorted reflection of his own face. When he finally looks at me, the father is gone; the CEO is there, but cracked.

"Do you know how many IPOs die because the story is boring?" he asks. "We are building aircraft that change how the world moves. Clean. Quiet. Safer. But it's not enough. The market is a god that wants blood." He laughs, but there's zero humor behind it. "And so we fed it a ghost. A crisis that looked like danger but never was."

I stare at him, motionless.

"Publicity," he says, as if tasting the word and finding it rancid now. "Momentum. A narrative. Our PR firm connected me with… with a firm that specializes in manufacturing urgency. They proposed something 'controlled'—mild threats, online chatter, security 'concerns' that would put us on screens as a company that takes safety seriously.

We agreed to precisely defined boundaries. No weapons. No contact. Ever."

My heartbeat is a bomb timer—beep, beep, beep—slowing, growing louder.

"What firm," I say.

"Kestrel Risk Solutions," he says. "Marcus Vale introduced me—he's my partner on the roadshow. The fired COO—Spencer DeLuca—put us in the same room as Kestrel's fixer. We were promised the narrative would elevate the share price by twenty percent."

Every muscle in my neck turns to wire. "The letters. The cardstock. The staged break-in."

He nods once, miserably. "The paper came from a list Kestrel gave us—obscure boutique stock, distinctive for recognition by... by your people." He swallows. "It spun out. After the mural incident, I throttled it and said we were done. Vale insisted the 'arc' needed one more crescendo. I refused. He... he found someone else."

"Who?" I whisper, even though I know. The partner who wants red.

"Vale engaged a freelancer Kestrel had blacklisted. Name I heard was Rourke. Ex-military, fired for using live rounds on a drill." He grips the edge of the desk until his knuckles bleach. "Yesterday I told Vale if anything else happened I'd burn his funds live on CNBC. We shouted. He laughed. Today… Camille is gone."

The room tilts. My promise to Cam—*keep you whole*—burns like a brand.

"Why tell me now?" I ask, and it's not kind. "Why not before my team risked their lives for a lie you helped start?"

He drops into his chair as if his legs gave out. When he looks up his eyes are wet. "Because I love my daughter. Because I thought I could control a fire and instead I lit one under a monster. Because I needed someone capable of ending this who wouldn't waste time lecturing me on ethics while my child was taken."

I want to break him. I want to walk around the desk, take him by his tie, and tell him what it feels like to watch a woman fight in a patch of grass while you arrive sixty seconds too late. But that won't bring her back.

I put my palms flat on his desk and lean in. "You are going to give me everything. Every email. Every burner number. Every contract. Every payment. Every Kestrel address."

He nods fast, rummages in a drawer, produces a folder too thick to be an accident. "I started compiling when they placed the bomb," he says, voice fraying. "There's a shell company—Alder Street Holdings—that Vale funneled payments through. Kestrel invoices came from a P.O. box in Magnolia Ridge. Rourke's last known was… a warehouse lease in South Ridgeville. Under another shell: Red Trace Logistics."

I snap photos, slide the files into my bag, and pin him with a stare. "Do not talk to the press. Do not call Vale. Do not breathe outside this room unless I tell you. If you go off script again, I will not be able to save you from Hartley."

He nods, swallowed whole by fear.

I'm at the door when he speaks again. "Bring her home."

I don't answer. If I open my mouth right now, the only word that will come out is a growl.

I head to the command room, my thoughts a swirl of anger and confusion. Riggs shuts the door as I enter, and leans back hard. "Jesus."

I hand him the folder. "Gregory started it. Vale escalated. A blacklisted Kestrel operative named Rourke is free-lancing now. We have a P.O. Box, a shell, and a likely warehouse in South Ridgeville operating under Red Trace."

Rae swears softly. "Son of a— That's why the threats had a mix of amateur and pro hallmarks. Two different hands."

"Dean is going to implode," Riggs mutters, flicking through invoices. "Controlled crisis my ass."

My satphone vibrates. Dean—already on. "Gregory is behind this? And he just told you?"

"He told me," I say. "Sending you the file now."

Sawyer

I beam the scan. Dean goes quiet as data scrolls on his end. He exhales something that could kill small animals. "Here's the plan," he says, calm and lethal. "We split capabilities. Riggs, you lock Kingsley House down and keep PD and Hartley inside the net—no leaks. Rae, you pivot to finance: run Alder Street Holdings through every payment processor; follow wires to physical addresses. Sawyer, you're point on Rourke. We'll loop in a trusted federal contact, but you move faster than paper does. You get a grid, you move. You do not breach alone."

"Copy," we echo in chorus.

Rae flips a screen to a map. "Alder Street's incoming wires show cashouts at three ATMs in Evermore two weeks running. Red Trace leases two units at a storage complex in South Ridgeville—Riverfront Industrial—units 312 and 314. One shows energy spikes at irregular intervals—somebody's running tools."

Riggs taps his chin. "Storage units are kidnapping 101. Sound masks, easy access, nobody asks questions."

I look at the clock. **14:27**. If the van took 115 south and exited near Fox Hollow, they could be there now.

"Hartley?" I ask.

Rae shakes her head. "He's Good Cop on Gregory. We shove him a slice, and we take the meat."

Dean grunts approval. "SPPD will want to own the collar, but I want Cam breathing, not a ribbon-cutting. Sawyer—bring two, not ten. Quiet over show."

"Riggs and Rae," I say. "And Anderssen on cordon if we get a second location."

Dean: "I'll have Orange-Plus on standby as QRF six minutes out. Make the hit clean."

I snap the mag in my SIG, and rack the slide. "We go now."

Riggs's eyes flare. "That's the look you get before doing something dumb and glorious."

"Who says it's dumb?" I check the holster retention, and grab a short-barrel carbine from the locker. "It's only dumb if we miss."

Rae's tablet chirps. "Wait—one more breadcrumb. The van—if they used a jammer, they might have turned it off when they parked. I'm seeing a white panel on a municipal cam, timestamp fifteen minutes ago, turning into the exact industrial park the lease lists. Partial plate matches outline. I'm ninety percent."

My pulse steadies—not calm, not joy—something colder.

"Gear up," I say. "We drive."

The SUV travels southbound, sirens nowhere near us, because this is off-books. The River glints on our right;

Sawyer

cranes needle the sky. My phone hums; Vanessa: Any word? I don't answer. My hands are busy strangling the steering wheel.

Riggs readies a breaching kit—bolt cutters, wedge, flex cuffs. Rae checks a trauma pouch, then toggles a drone to manual and sets it in a foam cradle—launch on arrival.

"Talk to me," Riggs says without looking up.

"Rourke," I say, spitting the name like a tooth. "Ex-military. Likes toys—jammer, flash-bang. Hates boundaries. Vale wanted a crescendo; Rourke took the whole orchestra."

"Motivation?" Rae asks. "Money? Leverage?"

"Control," I say. "Men like him jerk on strings because they like the dance."

"And Gregory," Riggs says, voice knifing dry. "You gonna punch him later?"

"I'm going to deliver his daughter breathing and then decide whether my fist needs a conversation." I glance in the mirror, catch my own eyes—cold, unblinking. "Right now he's a problem for tomorrow."

Rae flicks me a look. "Cam's going to be wrecked."

"I know."

The words scrape like gravel. I said I'd keep her whole. If

I'm too late, the thing in my chest that's just starting to believe in a future will cauterize shut.

We arrive at Riverfront Industrial. A grid of anonymous beige boxes and roll-up doors, numbers stenciled in stuttering logic. A few semis. Silence bouncing hard. We cruise once, eyes casual; Rae's drone lifts, slips high, owl-quiet. A white panel van sits crooked near Unit 312, nose pointed out. My mouth goes dry. Passenger door low-dent. A peeling orange triangle sticker clings near the bottom seam.

Rae whispers, "Gotcha."

"License plate?" Riggs asks.

"Paper temp. No state emblem. Fake."

"Heat signatures?" I murmur.

She checks the IR overlay. "Two, maybe three bodies in 312. 314's cold. One heat goes vertical then crouches. Could be on a mezzanine."

I park two buildings down, behind a stack of pallets. We gear. Gloves. Nods. We move—fast and low. At the corner, I hold up a fist. We freeze. A man in coveralls smokes beside Unit 318, completely oblivious. Riggs angles his body, hiding our kit. We slip past in the echo of a truck backfiring three blocks over.

At 312, paint flakes from the padlock. I can smell bleach and rubber and the faint iron of fear. My fear. Hers.

Sawyer

I tilt my head toward Rae. She lowers the drone, perches it on a gutter for an overwatch view.

Riggs positions on the hinge side with bolt cutters, and I crouch lock-side with the wedge. My ear to the metal. There's a murmur, a shift, and then a muffled thump. I close my eyes; there's a sound I know better than any: Cam's breath when she's holding it to stop tears.

I nod. Three… two… one.

Riggs bites the lock as I set the wedge and crank. Metal shrieks. The door jumps. I rip it up and duck left as a shape barrels forward—Rourke or not, I don't care—he hits the wedge, stumbles while reaching for his belt—flash-bang—no you don't—I shoulder into him, drive him into the concrete, my forearm pinning his throat as his fingers fumble the pin.

"Hands," Riggs roars, boot stamping the man's wrist. Bone cracks. The pin skitters. We shove the canister under the rolling door; it detonates outside, light and sound bleeding harmlessly into the lot.

Another figure lunges from the back—skinny, fast. Rae plants him to the ground with a knee in the spine and a zip tie that sings shut.

"Cam!" I shout, moving into the dim.

She's there.

On the floor against a stack of crates, wrists tied, tape smeared across her mouth, eyes red and bright but *alive*. The scream that detonates behind my ribs is the opposite of fear; it's something older, wilder.

I'm at her in three steps. I cut the zip ties, peel the tape gently, hissing when it takes a layer of skin. She gasps, chokes, then grabs my neck like a lifeline. I tuck her under my chin and breathe her in—turpentine, salt, and glue. My Cam.

"I'm here," I say, again and again, until her shaking slows enough for words.

"I counted turns," she whispers against my throat, voice shredded but fierce. "I tried to make it loud. I—"

"You did good." I cradle her face in my hands, pressing my forehead to hers. "You lit the sky."

Riggs cuffs the broken-wrist goon, who is moaning through a mask. "Rourke?" he asks.

I lift the mask. The face is a stranger. A hired nothing. "Where is he?" I snarl into the man's sweaty fear. "Where's Rourke?"

"No names, man," he pants. "We just—just a pickup."

"Who hired you? Vale?" My grip tightens.

He can't answer with the air cut off. I ease enough to let words through.

"We get cash, that's it. GPS pings; we drive. Warehouse number comes in an hour before. That's all. Please—my hand—"

"Good," I say, softly. "It hurts."

Rae stalks over, eyes predator-sharp. "We'll find your boss," she says. "You'll sing louder later."

Sirens begin to wail in the distance—Hartley, or CHP, or both—drawn by the flash of the munition and the drone's ping. I gather Cam, lift her, and her legs wrap around my waist like they're remembering something we promised last night.

"Home," she whispers.

"Home," I echo, and my voice breaks.

I carry her into the sun.

We'll figure the rest—the partner who played with matches, the fixer who wants fire, the father who finally told the truth. I'll hand the folder to Dean, and he'll peel Vale like fruit. Hartley will build a case. Rourke will get his day with my hands.

But right now, in the parking lot of a storage facility that looks like a thousand others, I hold the woman I almost lost and let the fact that she's breathing into my neck turn me human again.

"Rae," I say, already thinking seven moves ahead even as I feel Cam's pulse returning to calm under my thumb, "call Dean. Tell him we've got Cam and two live. Tell him the name Vale is coming off my lips with receipts."

"Copy," she says, voice fierce with satisfaction. "And Sawyer?"

"Yeah."

"Good hunt."

I kiss the top of Cam's head and start walking us toward the SUV. Behind us, Riggs reads the skinny perp his rights, and the drone hums like a satisfied hornet. Ahead: answers. A storm. And after that—if we survive the truth—blue paint, a studio floor, and a life I will put my body between and anything that tries to break it.

22

Camille

Hospitals always smell like lemon-bleach and boiled linens, like somebody tried to scrub life into something that forgot how to breathe. The ceiling over my bed hums with fluorescent daylight even though it's well past noon. A blood-pressure cuff kisses my arm every six minutes as if it can squeeze fear out of the arteries it helped flood.

I'm wearing a gown the color of regret and a warm blanket that never warms all the way. Tape rash blooms along my cheekbone where silver adhesive ripped my skin. The nurse with honey-brown braids keeps offering me ice chips. I take them because they're the only thing that doesn't taste like duct tape and panic.

Sawyer is a silhouette in a vinyl chair, boots planted, shoulders squared, headset in, phone face-down for once. He's said maybe twenty words to me since we got here—most of them not about me: to the triage nurse ("mild head trauma, tape abrasion, possible sprain left wrist"), to Detective Hartley ("we'll do the statement once scans clear"), to Dean through that deceptively ordinary phone ("we have the file; sending the whole rotten tree"). The rest he says with hands—the ones that found me in a concrete room—and eyes that won't stay still, bouncing from door to clock to drip line to me, back to the door.

"Your CT looks clear," the physician says, flipping a tablet at my bedside. He's young, probably my age, with a ring-shaped divot on his ring finger where a glove bit down during residency. "Concussion symptoms minimal. Tape burn we can treat. You'll be sore." His eyes lift to Sawyer. "No evidence of… anything else."

Relief punches my diaphragm from the inside. I nod. "Can I go home?"

"We'd like to observe you for a few hours," he says. "Detective Hartley's waiting to take a statement if you feel up to it."

"Later," Sawyer answers for me, voice sanded down to control. He stands, shakes the doctor's hand. "Thanks, Doc."

The doctor exits. The nurse helps me peel gauze from my cheek. Tears threaten and I grip the rails hard enough to squeak the plastic because I refuse to cry over adhesive. Crying is for actual things, like the moment the van door

Sawyer

closed and the world shrank to stink and dark and the sound of my heart learning how to be a hammer.

"You should try to rest," the nurse murmurs, patting my shoulder. She leaves us alone with the ceiling hum.

Sawyer takes the chair again. He's so close I could reach out and brush the hardened scar near his collarbone if I wanted. I don't. I can't. There's a tightness in his mouth I don't recognize, a secret lodged like a pebble under the tongue.

"What aren't you telling me?" I ask.

The muscles along his jaw leap. He looks at the door instead of me. "We'll talk when you're resting."

"I'm resting." I gesture at the cannula taped to my hand, the beeping monitor counting my every spike. "Talk."

He exhales through his nose, the way he does right before he picks a wire to cut. "Hartley wants to take your statement before we—"

I snap. "Sawyer."

His attention snaps with me. For a second the soldier falls off and the man shows; it hurts more, seeing him bare and bracing.

"Okay," he says. Careful. "First: the text that got you to the garden wasn't your father. It was spoofed."

My lungs let out air I didn't realize was hoarded. It explains the wrongness, the prickle. "Then who—?"

He swallows. His eyes flicker—hallway, IV pole, my face—calculating angles. "Someone used a contact they knew you'd trust to get you outside."

"Someone inside," I say, because he's trained me to follow threads. "Someone who knew which name would move me."

"Yes."

He doesn't keep going. I can feel the rest of it in the room like electromagnetic vibrato, rattling the bed rails. "That's not the pebble," I say. "Say it."

He rubs the heel of his hand once over his sternum, a soldier's tell I've learned to read. "Cam…" He sits forward, elbows on knees, head bowed like a man about to pray to a god he doesn't believe in. "Your father made a deal. Months ago. To create… a controlled security narrative around the company and—" His throat tightens. He forces the next words out. "—around you."

I flinch so hard the blood-pressure cuff thinks it's a crisis. It starts to inflate. I rip it off with my free hand.

"What does that mean?" The question comes out brittle and quiet at the same time.

"PR. Manufactured urgency. The firm staged mild threats—paper notes, online chatter—to boost the story before the IPO. No contact. No weapons. Your father says he pulled the plug after the first breach. His partner—Vale—ignored him. Hired a freelancer named Rourke. It escalated out of control."

The ceiling hum surges. Or maybe that's my skull filling with bees. I stare at him, shaking my head in a slow motion that tries to erase everything he said syllable by syllable.

"No," I say. "No. He wouldn't." Words scramble over each other, tripping. "My father is—he's ridiculous about optics and shareholders and who sits where at the gala, yes, but he wouldn't—" My voice splits. "He wouldn't use me like that."

Sawyer doesn't reach for me. He's learned the shape of my edges. "He admitted it," he says.

"Liar," I snap, not sure if I mean my father or Sawyer. That's how bad it is.

He doesn't flinch. "He thought it would stay staged. He says he tried to stop it. Vale—the partner—went outside the plan. Brought in a guy blacklisted for going hot. Cam, I'm not defending him. I'm telling you the chain so we can break it."

I hear him. I don't hear him. My bones hear him, but my skin refuses.

"That text said my father's name." Tears breach despite every command I give them to stand down. "It was him."

"It was his ghost." He swallows. "Spoofed to look like him. Because the real him made it plausible."

The nurse peeks in, reading the volume and our faces the way nurses do. She retreats silently and I hate that she saw us like this.

"Get my dad," I say, voice low and lethal. "I want to see him."

"Cam…"

"Get. Him." A thousand memories line up behind the command: Gregory pushing me higher on the tire swing, Gregory attending my middle school 'art show' in the cafeteria and buying every macaroni frame for ten dollars each, Gregory calling me Pumpkin in front of *everyone* and me cringing because Dad and love and embarrassment are synonyms when you're fourteen. People aren't simple. They're messy. But they don't weaponize you for stock prices. They don't.

Sawyer stands, the chair legs scraping. He looks bigger and further away all at once. "Hartley's with him. They'll arrange it. But before he walks in—"

"I don't want before." My voice breaks. "I want him."

He nods once, a tactical retreat. He steps toward the door and hesitates. "I'm on your side," he says, his voice raw and threadbare.

Sawyer

"Are you?" It knifes out before I can sheath it. "Because it feels like you've been keeping this to yourself while you… while you held me like I was—" I slam my eyes shut. The image hurts—my face in his neck, my breath in his shirt, the word *always* tattooing promises on ribs that feel bruised from the inside.

He doesn't defend himself. "I found out not long ago," he says. "At your house. In your father's office. I needed to verify before I put pain in your mouth."

"Too late," I whisper, and the worst part is I'm not sure where to aim the hurt. It ricochets, hitting everything. Him. Me. My father. The ceiling.

There's a knock. Detective Hartley's face appears round the curtain, tie askew, expression carefully neutral. "Miss Kingsley," he says. "Good to see you upright. We'll take this slow. Your father is in a consult room with my partner. Would you like to speak to him?"

"Yes," I say immediately. "Now."

"We'll keep it supervised," Hartley adds gently.

I look at Sawyer. He is made of restraint again, ironed back up, hands hooked on his belt like he wants to use them and won't. "Stay," I hear myself say, then hear what I said and claw it back. "No. Go. I can't—" I shake my head, flailing for space. "I can't do this with you looking at me like—like you already know how it ends."

Something flickers in his eyes—hurt, then understanding, then that maddening acceptance that makes me want to kiss him and punch him in the same breath. "I'll be right outside," he says anyway.

"I said go." I don't mean *go away forever.* I mean *go out of my line of sight before I drown.*

He nods once, and it lands like a salute. He steps past Hartley without looking back. The curtain sways in his wake.

The room is suddenly too big, or I am too small inside it. The machines beep the way games used to when I was allowed to be only a kid. My cheeks are wet. I wipe them with the heel of my hand and it stings—the tape burn, the stupid fragile skin that never asked to be the stage for anyone's PR stunt.

Hartley clears his throat. "Do you need a minute?"

"No." If I stop moving I will rot. "Bring him."

He disappears. I try to slow my breath the way Sawyer taught me—four in, four out—but all I can hear is the rush of a van's engine and all I can see is a white rectangle of sky framed by cargo doors.

I twist the hospital bracelet on my wrist until the plastic bites. The ink bleeds: *KINGSLEY, CAMILLE*— as if I needed reminding who I am.

Sawyer

The curtain rattles. My father steps in with Hartley. He looks smaller in fluorescent light, his hair mussed, tie loose, eyes rimmed in sleepless red. He stops six feet from the bed like it's the edge of a cliff.

"Pumpkin." His voice breaks on the word.

I nearly laugh because it's so wildly wrong and tender and infuriating I could scream. "Did you text me," I ask, calm as the moment before a shatter, "to meet you in the south garden?"

He blinks. "No," he says quickly. "No, sweetheart, I would never—"

"But you set the stage where a text like that would feel normal." The calm peels away. "You hired a company to scare me so Wall Street would clap for you."

He flinches like I slapped him. "Who told you—"

"I didn't hear it from the gossip rags, Dad," I spit. "I heard it from the man who found me tied like a package in a storage unit. So—answer me. Did you?"

His mouth opens. Closes. He looks at Hartley like the detective might throw him a rope. Hartley's face is granite. My father looks back at me. "I thought it would be controlled," he says, words spilling, desperate. "No one was supposed to touch you. I pulled out when it went too far—"

"But only after it started." My hands shake. "Only after you lit the fuse."

He presses his fingers to his eyes and for a second I see the man who taught me to ride a bike and bled with me when I fell. "I'm sorry," he says into his palm. He drops his hand and the CEO returns for a beat. "I will fix it. I will make him pay."

"Which him?" I ask. My voice has turned wrong. It's the calm before the final storm, the eye. "The man you paid to light a fake fire? The partner who threw gas? Or the one who used me as kindling?"

He sways. "All of them."

I inhale like I'm drawing air through a straw in tar. "Get out." The words arrive before I know they exist. They surprise me. They fit.

"Camille—"

"Get. Out." I point at the curtain because I have to point at something that isn't his face. "I can't—" My throat closes around how much I can't. "Hartley can take your statement in the hallway or in hell; I don't care where. I will talk to you when I can hear myself think without hearing the van doors."

Hartley moves him gently by the elbow. Gregory lets himself be steered, stunned and gray. At the curtain he turns back. "I love you," he says, and I want to throw the heart monitor at him because that word feels like counterfeit currency he used in a place that only takes cash.

They're gone. The room fills with fluorescent and beeping and that lemon-bleach again like a stupid hymn.

I fold in on myself. Not a ball, because my hip aches and the IV tubing tethers me, but some smaller shape. I drag the warm blanket up and it smells like a hundred other people who were scared here before me. It doesn't help. I bury my face in it and breathe until breaths stop clawing.

Through the thin curtain I hear low voices—Hartley, clinical and inexorable; my father, smaller and smaller. Somewhere, a door opens. Somewhere, a pen scratches ruin onto paper.

I think of Sawyer in the hallway. I think of the way his eyes softened when he said *always* and the way they hardened when he said *we finish it*. I think of the sticky note I pinned to his chest—*trust your gut*—and wonder if I can obey my own handwriting when my gut is an ocean churning.

A soft shadow falls across the curtain. "It's just me," comes his voice, low and careful.

"Go away," I say, because love is a thing with edges and mine is flayed to ribbons. "Please."

A beat. "I'll be right outside," he says.

"I know." It isn't forgiveness. It isn't anything yet. It's just a fact. He leaves footsteps in air where there should be floor.

I stare at my paint-stained cuticles. They look like somebody else's hands, somebody else's life. I flex them, feeling tender skin pull. Color can't cover blood. I know that now. But maybe, when the blood dries, color can make a map. Later. Not yet.

For now, I lie under the hospital light and let the ache expand until it's as big as the sky. I let the truth sit, sour and heavy, because it's better than the lie that almost killed me. I let myself hate and love the same two men in different measures that change with every beep.

And I wait for the next breath to come without breaking.

23

Sawyer

Hospitals are built from two materials: antiseptic and time. The antiseptic burns your nose; the time gets under your nails. I take up my station on a plastic chair outside Cam's room and count the flicker in the fluorescents until I know exactly when the ballast in the fourth light down the hall is going to stutter. It's every forty-seven seconds. The pulse lines up with the steady ping of a telemetry monitor two rooms over and the intermittent squeak of a med cart with a bad wheel.

It shouldn't help. It does. Patterns mean I'm not thinking about the way she said *go* without saying *away*, the way her mouth trembled when I told her what her father did, the way I couldn't bring myself to reach for her when everything in me wanted to.

I'm close enough to the door that if she called my name I'd hear it through a blanket. Far enough that I'm not breaking the last instruction she gave me. That's the line I'm walking now: the width of a hallway, the height of a vow.

Riggs texts a photo of a whiteboard in our mobile command app—the case board reproduced in markers. At the center: VALE in red underlined twice. Radiating spokes: Kestrel Risk (subhead: "front office, Magnolia Ridge P.O. box"), Alder Street Holdings ("shell/ACH funnel"), Red Trace ("South SP units 312/314"), Rourke ("ex-mil, blacklisted, current location unknown"), Perps #1/#2 ("lawyered, giving us crumbs"), Gregory ("cooperating; secured"). In the corner Rae added a doodle of a little triangle sticker peeling off a van. The caption says: *peels like a scab.*

I send back: *Good. Keep pushing Alder—follow every wire.* Then I pocket the phone when a nurse rounds the corner with Cam's chart. She's seen me enough times today to stop jumping when she notices the large man with the permanent scowl and the neck mic.

"She's resting," she says softly. "Vitals are good. She asked for water. We're keeping it sips for now."

"Thanks," I say. "I'm five feet away if she needs anything."

The nurse studies me. The look isn't romantic or suspicious. It's the look of someone who's moved a thousand families through this hallway and can tell when a man's chain of custody on his own heart is precarious. "We'll keep the press off this floor," she says. "Security briefed us."

"Appreciate it," I tell her. I mean it.

My satphone buzzes in my pocket. Dean.

"Status?" he asks with no preamble.

"Cam's cleared medically but they're holding her for observation. Her statement will wait until she can breathe without tasting duct tape. Perps one and two are in a fifth-floor interview at SPPD, lawyers present. Hartley's walking them through a plea ladder. Gregory confessed the controlled-crisis scheme, named Vale and Kestrel, handed over a file thick enough to choke a wood chipper. We found the Riverfront unit, got Cam back. Rourke is still dirt we haven't shaken out of the rug."

"I've got a fed at Main Justice who owes me," Dean says. "SEC, FBI, and USAO are salivating over the market manipulation angle. They'll squeeze Vale on wire fraud and conspiracy to commit kidnapping even if he never touched a van. We're pushing ex parte warrants for Kestrel's accounts and a Title III on Vale's current phones."

"Timeline?"

"Judge is in chambers now," Dean says. I can hear boots on concrete behind him—he's moving. "Ninety minutes for paper we can use. Until then, sit on him without spooking.

He's at a mid-day at his VC pal's office in SoMa. Orange Team has eyes on the lobby."

"Rourke?"

"Whispers he was seen around a body shop in Lighthouse Point that doubles as a toy box for mercs. Name's *Hatch Auto & Marine*. It's where you go if you need your boat transponder to suddenly die. The owner's a vet with a code, but he hates freelancers who make him look bad."

"Send me the address," I say, heart rate ticking up into the zone that makes me useful. "Riggs can bounce on it."

"You're staying with Cam," Dean says, reading my mind and closing the door to the reckless part of it. "I want you there when she comes up for air. Riggs is already en route with Rae. This is a two-prong: we cap Vale with paper and keep Rourke from flipping the board again. Copy?"

"Copy," I say, and watch a janitor buff the floor in slow hypnotic ovals that reflect the ceiling back up at me like a weird, inverted lake.

Hartley appears ten minutes later, tie loosened, jaw tight. He nods to me like a man who's chosen alliance over ego and doesn't mind me knowing it. "She all right?"

"Resting," I say. "You'll get your statement when she's ready."

He looks like he wants to argue. He doesn't. "We've got counsel on your pair from Riverfront. One's giving us logistics: coded texts with drop locations, cash pick-ups, one-time numbers. The other—broken wrist—just found religion. He says the guy he called 'Boss' never used Rourke's name, but he did use a phrase: *Red star, canvas bleed.* Ring any bells?"

"Perp's poetry," I say grimly. "He's been sending us color metaphors since the first letter." I pause. "What about Vale?"

"Meeting with his attorneys as we speak," Hartley says dryly. "But wheels are moving. Your boss's friend at Justice has more juice than the espresso downstairs."

"He's not my boss," I say automatically, then concede with a tilt of my head. "He's my cousin who keeps my leash long enough to run."

Hartley almost smiles. "You're going to love what my CSU found taped under the Riverfront unit's table."

"Tell me."

"GPS jammer, yes. Flash-bang casings, yes. Also a little nest for a phone with a SIM that pings a prepaid at—wait for it—a co-working space in the Fox Hollow. The same neighborhood your shell company's ATMs saw Alder's cash-outs."

"Rae's already on Fox Hollow," I say. "We'll cross numbers."

He pats the chart he's not supposed to have, because he's a detective and rules are flexible when heartbeats are on the line. "She's tough," he says, eyes softening. "When she talks, I'm going to need you to give her space."

"She already took it," I say, and the words taste like penance.

After he leaves, I stand because I've sat too long and the energy has nowhere to go. I pace the length of the hallway and back, hands folded behind me tight enough that the tendon in my left wrist clicks. On my third pass, a blur of green silk and perfume hits the T-intersection, heels skidding.

"Where is she?" Vanessa demands, hair wild, sunglasses fogging. Her gaze bounces off my chest and shoulders like she's trying to climb me with eyes. "They wouldn't tell me her room!"

"Keep it down," I say, holding up a palm. "She's resting. Hartley will let you in once she says yes."

She plants fists on hips. "I'm on her yes list."

"And I'm on the list that keeps the world small right now," I say. "You'll make it bigger."

Vanessa deflates an inch. "Is she… is she hurt?"

I shake my head. "Mostly scrapes. Scared." I weigh what else to say, decide honesty will help us both. "Gregory talked."

Sawyer

Her jaw drops. "He— No. He wouldn't."

"He did," I say, not softly. "And I'm not the one you need to yell that at."

She looks at me like maybe I'm a door she could both kick and lean on. Then she sighs, pulls her sunglasses off, and the streaks of mascara under her eyes aren't staged. "Tell my girl I'm here," she says, voice gentled. "Tell her I'm not going anywhere."

"Will do," I say. She squeezes my forearm in a gesture that says thanks and sorry and don't you dare screw this up, then stalks down the hall to find coffee she can weaponize.

My phone vibrates in my pocket.

Riggs: Hatch Auto & Marine is a warren. Owner (Hatcher) says he hasn't seen Rourke in three days, but a Riverfront-style jammer was serviced here last week. Rae pulled shop cams: guy in ball cap, beard, scar on left ear. Hatcher calls him "Bane." Could be our man.

I text back: If Hatcher's a vet with a code, we can push him without breaking him. Offer him an IOU he actually values: getting Rourke off his stoop.

Riggs: Already working him. Rae's scraping "Bane" through data brokers.

Rae pings the thread with a still from the shop cam: a man in a ball cap caught mid-turn, leaving a sliver of his face and the edge of a distinctive ear notch. "Pulled from a

2018 bar fight, dishonorable discharge records under 'Evan Rourke' show a similar injury," she writes. "Also: cellphone tower pings from a prepaid that hit Fox Hollow co-working two nights in a row after midnight, then Lighthouse Point in the morning. Breadcrumbs. I'm on him."

Across the hall, the fluorescents thrift and flare: forty-seven seconds. The metronome of the fourth light. Still there. So am I.

I pull my notebook—the paper one, not the encrypted app—and write names and verbs because I have learned over and over that sometimes you have to put ink next to a plan if you want it to become something you can hold.

- **Marcus Vale** — Atlantic Heights townhouse + SoMa office. *Surveil. Serve warrants. Freeze Alder & personal accounts. Seize devices before they're wiped. Get travel logs: jet tail numbers; watch for flight to no-extradition.*
- **Kestrel Risk** — Magnolia Ridge P.O. Box + call center. *Subpoena client list; seize CRM; flip low-level staff; show them kidnapping enhancement sentencing guidelines.*
- **Rourke / "Bane"** — Hatch Auto & Marine + Fox Hollow co-working. *Canvas camera rings. Make it too hot to move. Box him. Choose the arrest space to protect collateral (no civilians, clear backstop).*
- **Inside assist** — text spoof + contact knowledge.

Sawyer

> *Gregory's assistant? PR firm? Caterer assignment editor? Cross-ref who had Cam's inner circle numbers.*
> - **Cam** — privacy protocol. *Alias on chart. Two Orange at both ends of corridor. Decoy discharge route if press gets frisky.*

I close the book and lean my head against the wall. The paint is cool. The cinderblock under it is older than I am. I tell myself I'm letting the building hold up some of the weight.

A cough from inside brings me upright. I don't open the door. I don't call her name. I put my palm against the wood directly over where I know her bed is—she likes to sleep with her head toward the window when she can. I don't push. Just… anchor. It's ridiculous. It steadies me anyway.

"Mr. Maddox?" Hartley again. He keeps his voice low. "We just got a heads-up: your boy Vale's counsel is trying to get him wheels-up to Vegas 'for meetings.' We're about twenty minutes from warrants."

"Vegas is a hop to anywhere," I say. "We can't lose him. You got a legal way to sit on him until paper lands?"

"We can do a 'consensual conversation' that takes fifteen minutes and a lot of coffee," he says, mouth twisting. "Or we can get lucky with code compliance on his office and have someone 'notice' an occupancy issue."

"Do both," I say. "I'll call Dean to have the fed bark."

He snorts. "Thought you'd say that."

By the time I loop Dean in, his friend in the Bureau has already leaned on Vale's counsel. A polite but ironclad "do not travel" request is now in writing. The kind that says "your boarding pass will print, but the men in windbreakers will meet you at the gate." It's not an arrest. It's a glare that buys us an hour.

Rae drops a new pin in our shared map. *Fox Hollow—co-working. "Bane" logged in as "Stark" last night (they cross-sell day passes online). IP address used to access a single page: municipal police scanner feed and a Craigslist posting for storage units near the airport.* She adds: *He's compulsive about checking his own myth.* Then: *Hatcher likes us. He just texted an address on Third Street where Rourke sleeps when he's between jobs. Cheap monthly. Unit 4B. We're rolling.*

"Riggs—do not hit 4B without me," I say into the line, even as I know I can't go. The words taste like broken teeth.

"I'll put eyes and wait for the paper," he promises. "Rae'll give me a door cam in five. If he moves, I shadow."

"Good," I say. "If he spooks, don't escalate. I want him alive to point at Vale."

"You also want his teeth," Riggs says mildly.

"I'll settle for his phone," I lie, because we both know I want both.

The fourth light flickers. Forty-seven seconds. Somewhere down the hall, a code page barks and slams through a different set of doors; an emergency we aren't in. For once.

Gregory appears at the far end of the corridor like a ghost who got lost. He moves with the hesitance of a man who knows he isn't welcome and wants to be punished for it. Hartley slots into place at his shoulder before I have to stand. He's good at his job. I don't move, except to tighten my hand into a fist on my knee.

Gregory stops a polite distance away. His eyes are a color softer than Cam's but I can see the gene. "Is she—?"

"Resting," I say.

He nods as if he deserved a different answer. He opens his mouth, shuts it again, opens it. "I'm going to turn over my phone to Detective Hartley. Everything. I've already called my general counsel," he says, deflated. "And I scheduled a press conference for tomorrow to apologize to the community—"

"Cancel it," I cut in, low, because the thought of Cam's pain being chewed by cameras makes bile flood my mouth. "If you stand at a podium right now, you turn a target into a spectacle. Sit with law enforcement. Sit with your shame. Leave the podium until Cam isn't the headline."

He flinches. "I thought transparency—"

"Transparency is telling your daughter with your own mouth before she hears it from a man she's paid to trust," I say, and even I hear the acid. "You missed that window. Don't miss this one."

Hartley steers him away again. I exhale and realize my shoulders are somewhere around my ears. I drop them one notch at a time.

The nurse returns with a fresh bag of saline. She glances at me, at the way my hands want to punch and pray simultaneously. "She asked me to tell you something," she says.

I straighten before I can stop myself. "Is she…?"

"She's not ready to see you." The nurse smiles gently when my face betrays more than I want it to. "But she said to tell you she heard you at the door."

"What did I say?" I ask, wrong-footed.

"Nothing," the nurse says. "That's the point."

I swallow. It lands like glass and I don't care.

My phone vibrates in a staccato I've set aside for one thing only: incoming **GO** texts from Riggs. I step to the window to read.

RIGGS: Eyes on 4B. "Bane" present—ball cap, ear nick, same build. He's packing a duffel. Rae got warrants hot from Dean's guy. SPPD is two out. You sure you don't want to play?

I look at Cam's doorway and think of what she needs, not what I want.

ME: Bring him breathing.

RIGGS: Always.

I text Rae separately: Don't let SPPD burn the door. He'll badge at a window if they spook him. Quiet, surgical.

She thumbs a 👍 and adds: *Hatcher just sent me "Bane's" preferred coffee—there's a cart on the corner. I'm having the vendor call building security about a "spill" in the lobby to clear civilians. Don't say I never give you gifts.*

I almost smile. Almost.

The hall quiets in a way that isn't silence—it's the absence of footsteps that don't matter. Two Orange operators I posted at either end of the corridor trade a look with me that says *we've got this slice of earth*. A phlebotomist slips past, humming something that sounds like an old Motown track under her breath. The fourth light doesn't flicker on time. I notice and then it flickers anyway. Forty-eight seconds. Nothing is perfect. We move anyway.

Vanessa returns with enough coffee for a platoon and sets one beside my chair without comment. "Black, no sugar," she says. She doesn't ask how I like it; somehow she knows. Or she's watched me long enough to guess. "Tell her I'm here," she says again. Then she curls in a seat down the hall, legs folded, phone face-down, for once silent.

At 18:12 my satphone rings with Dean's brand of weary triumph. "Vale's phones are in a Faraday bag and he's discovering he's not half as clever as he thought," he says. "He's at the SPPD building with counsel, which means we have him in a box. Kestrel's P.O. box is a dead end with a live wire attached: a clerk saw a guy matching 'Bane' pick up mail twice this month. We're sending that across."

"And Rourke?"

"Riggs will tell you, but early word is that he's got a front row seat to the man discovering that his apartment door can be opened with a master key and a slapped warrant. Officers on scene say he was mid-duffel and not half as brave without a mask and a van."

I close my eyes.

Dean huffs out a, "You did good, Sawyer."

"Not good enough," I say. "Not yet."

"Then keep going," he says, and hangs up.

I text Riggs: **Status?** He sends a photo I will never show Cam—a blurred still of a bruise of a man face-down on rough carpet, cuffs on, the notch in his ear proof of identity. Another text follows: **Phone seized. SIMs. Two throwaways. One still warm. We'll get him to talk.**

Sawyer

I let my head hit the wall again, close my eyes, and for the first time since the van door slammed in my imagination and then in the world, I let my breath out all the way. The sound it makes is a rough thing. Vanessa hears it and pretends she didn't. One of the Orange operators looks away pointedly. The nurse smiles like a small moon.

Through the door I hear a rustle and the faintest *click* of a bed control. I don't move. I put my palm flat to the wood one more time and say nothing again.

A text glows on my screen. **Cam**: *I need time.*

My fingers hover. Then I type: *Take it. I'm outside.*

The dots appear. Disappear. Appear again. *Don't go far,* comes back.

Never, I send.

I pocket the phone, sit back down in the ugly chair, and let the antiseptic and time do what they do while we do what we do better: hunt, build, close. Because this is the part of war nobody likes to put in recruitment videos—waiting while the net tightens, while the warrants are served, while the man with the ear nick sits in a room under fluorescent hell and tells us where he hid the rest of the rot.

And when it's done—when Vale signs the last paper that names his sin, when Rourke points to the last locker—we'll walk out of here. Maybe not today. Maybe not tomorrow.

But we'll leave, and when we do, we won't be going back to the world we had before.

We'll build a new one. With doors that hold. With walls that don't need to be this thick to make us feel safe. With a table permanently stained with blue and copper and a laugh in a kitchen where the coffee doesn't taste like waiting.

But for now: I keep watch.

Forty-seven seconds. *Flicker.*

I'm here.

24

Camille

Hospitals measure time in drips and beeps. Back at the house, time is paint drying—slow at the edges, fast where you need it to last. Since they discharged me, I keep catching myself staring at ordinary things like they're evidence: a bread knife lying too close to the counter's edge, the way a shadow slices a doorway, the exact click of a lock I've heard a thousand times. My brain tags everything *threat/not threat*, the way Sawyer taught me, except now the sorting happens without permission.

Sawyer gives me space. He's here, yet not, like a star you can find even when you don't look at it directly. He'll linger in the hall until my breath evens, then vanish to answer a call. He walks the perimeter at dusk with Riggs, murmuring into his throat mic, and at sunrise I sometimes catch him on the veranda, coffee cooling by his boot while he scans the drive. He's a constant background hum that makes the rest of the sounds sort themselves out.

I'm not ready to let him back into the sphere where he was before. He knows it, accepts the distance like a man holding a weight at arm's length because the person beneath it asked him to.

So I paint.

The first canvas back is ugly on purpose—charcoal slashed with sickly green, aluminum gray smeared with the yellow of streetlights I didn't see but felt under my skin. I paint the ridges of a cargo van floor with the ribbed side of a palette knife, the way sound thudded through my jaw. Then, in the upper corner, almost invisible, I pull a single stroke of titanium white, thin as a breath. Sawyer's line. The first time he drew it, I thought: protection disguised as motion. Now it looks like a promise I held with my teeth.

Vanessa comes by on day two with Tupperware of arroz con pollo and a bag full of brightly colored scrunchies "for hospital-hair days you escaped but still deserve to accessorize." She perches on my studio stool and watches me paint until the urge to fill silence makes her burst.

"He should be in here," she declares after exactly twelve minutes, meaning Sawyer.

"He is," I say, gesturing to the line. "In a way."

Vanessa squints at the canvas, then at me. "You're doing that thing where you make metaphors so potent they turn into people."

"People made them first." I dab white into gray until the edge blooms. "He's giving me room."

"Which you want," she says gently, not a question. Vanessa can turn her voice into a blanket when she wants. "How's your dad?"

The breath leaves me like I've been punched. I keep my hand steady anyway. "He's… talking to anyone with a badge and a subpoena. He apologized." My mouth twists. "He keeps trying to find the words that don't exist."

"You'll find yours when you're ready," she says. "In the meantime, I brought gossip: Hartley has Vale by the portfolio."

That pulls my head up. "What happened?"

She grins wolfish. "Your soldier boy and his boss pulled strings in places that don't have strings, and suddenly the United States of Attorney People are very interested in a certain storytelling venture. Vale tried to fly to Vegas; the men in windbreakers met him at the jet. Kestrel Risk dissolved in a press release yesterday morning. Their co-owner is singing like an aria."

I smear blue into the ugly. "Rourke?"

"Arrested in Lighthouse Point." Her tone flattens. "Resisted. Guess who resisted back."

A tremor shoots through me, half fear, half heat that shouldn't belong with fear and does anyway when it's Sawyer we're talking about. "Is he—"

"Alive," she says. "Bruised. Charged with kidnapping, attempted aggravated assault, use of an explosive device at a public event—"

I nod.

"—and a bunch of words that sound like lawyers flexing," she finishes. "He has an arraignment tomorrow."

Rage tastes metallic under my tongue. I rinse my brush in turp and go back to work. "And the van?"

"Impounded." She shudders. "Saw a photo on a detective's tablet. Ugly inside. I wanted to drive a fist through things, and you know I don't punch."

That night, Sawyer updates me without pushing, standing in the doorway with his shoulder on the frame like he doesn't trust his hands near my paint. "Vale's devices gave us more than his lawyers want to admit," he says. "We found threads to the shell company, notes on Kestrel, and messages to a burner—the one Rourke carried. Hartley's ADA is building a conspiracy case that ties their 'story arc' to the escalation. Kestrel's co-owner is cooperating for a deal."

Sawyer

"And my father?" I ask, even though I don't want to.

"Not charged." His voice is careful, neutral like a nurse's hands. "Cooperating witness. He signed an affidavit detailing the scheme and his termination point. He's stepping aside from the roadshow, maybe the CEO seat for a while. He set up a fund for victims of stalking and manufactured harassment—yes, it's PR, but it also helps. He asked if he could see you."

I breathe once. "Not yet."

Sawyer nods. Neither pleased nor disappointed. Simply noting a waypoint. "Understood."

We fall into a rhythm that belongs to triage and repair. Mornings I paint, afternoons I meet with Detective Hartley to answer questions I can answer without making my pulse sprint. "You don't have to look at the photos," Hartley says, and I don't, not the bloody details or the angle of the hinge where the door met my shin. I do ask to see the orange triangle sticker. I stare at its torn corner for too long, letting my eyes memorize its peel. Every villain's choice is this dumb, I tell myself: something small they didn't think would matter. That helps and makes me furious in equal measure.

We find the inside assist too, and that one perforates something soft I didn't know was still intact. It wasn't my father's assistant—bless her iron spine—but a junior account exec at the PR firm who'd been tasked with "monitoring my channels." She sent Vale a spreadsheet labeled *INTEL—CAM PERS CONTACTS* the week before the gala: friends, vendors, staff, my father's patterns, and—buried halfway down like a nail under a rug—my cell. "Optimization," her email said. "In case we need nimble plays." Nimble plays. I almost throw the printout across Hartley's interview room, but I hand it back instead and watch the ADA put a neat paperclip on it like she's tacking a butterfly, as if that stops the wings from ever having flapped.

At night I climb into a bed that feels too big and too loud with memory. I dream about van doors and then, sometimes, about a thin white line that never lets the red touch me. When I wake at two or four, the hall light is a soft gold sliver under my door, and Sawyer's shadow sits with it like a patient dog. I don't ask him in. He doesn't press. My fingers ache to curl in his shirt anyway.

On the fourth day, Hartley calls while I'm rinsing brushes. "We've set the arraignments," he says. "Rourke today, Vale tomorrow morning. The judge is old school; he likes personal impact statements at bail. No pressure."

"I'm not ready," I say, throat thick. "This can't be about cameras again."

"It's not," Hartley says. "Your presence—silent—speaks to risk. A nod, a shake of the head. Or nothing at all. Your call."

Sawyer

I hang up and find Sawyer already at the doorway, as always, reading my face the way bomb techs read shadows. "You don't have to go," he says.

"I know," I say. "I think I need to see their faces once without masks."

At the courthouse, the air tastes like old paper, and voices pool under the marble ceiling like low thunder. I sit between Vanessa and Rae; Sawyer stands at the end of our pew, a pillar in a suit that makes him look like a better building. When they bring Rourke in, shackled, he scans the room and then drops his gaze mid-sweep when he hits me. I think: *Look at me.* He doesn't. He stares at a water stain on the floor like it's a map out. His lawyer talks about roots and jobs and the presumption of innocence. The ADA asks for remand without bail. I don't stand. I don't cry. When the judge denies bail, a breath I didn't realize I'd strapped down unbuckles.

Vale the next morning is all polish cracked at the edges. He arrives with a haircut, a pale navy suit, and the flustered entitlement of a man who's only ever been first on the golf tee. He scans for cameras and finds eyes. Mine. He jerks, and looks away. The ADA talks about money as leverage and crime. The judge listens with a face that belongs on coins. Bail is set like a number you need to choke on to learn a lesson. Vale nods as if he can pay any number. Later, I hear the freeze order hit his accounts, and the weight of that nod crushes him.

Between court and sleep, we finish something we started months ago: the downtown mural with the kids. Hartley posts two officers on the corner; the new day-to-day security company—HarborShield, local, discreet—sends two agents in polos that look like lifeguards to watch the crosswalk. Riggs elbows Sawyer, teasing that he and Rae are going to miss their celebrity detail; Rae flicks a paint dot on his sleeve like a salute. The kids arrive in a flurry of backpacks and squeals. They want to know how I escaped a "movie van." I tell them: knees and noise and never forgetting your name. Sawyer leans against a lamppost, arms folded, eyes on everything. When a third-grader named Addie asks him to hold her palette because her arms are tired, he does, solemnly, like she's entrusted him with the nuclear codes. I fall in love with him all over again from six feet away and then remember I asked for space. The ache and the heat share a bench in my chest.

Gregory shows up to the mural mid-afternoon with his tie off for the first time since I was eight. He stops at the tape line Sawyer quietly sets with his body. He doesn't cross it. "May I watch?" he asks, voice careful.

"It's a public wall," I say, dipping cobalt into sunlight.

"Your mother would have loved this," he says after a while, not quite to me. "She was the one who taught me how to look past the renderings and see the people in the building."

Sawyer

"I know," I say, because this is true and doesn't cancel anything else.

He doesn't press. Later, he sends word through Hartley that he'll be stepping aside officially, not just for the roadshow. Interim CEO. Voluntary testimony. Therapy. It's a nice string of words. I tuck them in a box labeled *we'll see* and close the lid for now.

The night before BRAVO breaks down their command trailer, we have a handover meeting at the dining table with the HarborShield lead—a man named Nathan with steady eyes and a binder full of practical. Edgar sits in, proud as if we're launching a new ship. Sawyer talks him through the protocols he designed: the QR code guest system, the blind spots we found and fixed, the way sound travels badly in the east hall but too well in the conservatory. He hands over a thumb drive of SOPs that could run a small nation. Nathan's pen scribbles like a hummingbird.

"Two agents on site at all times?" he confirms.

"Three, until the hearing," Sawyer says.

Nathan nods. "We're not Maddox, but we care about our clients."

"I know," I say, and see Sawyer's jaw notch.

When the meeting ends, Riggs and Rae disappear on errands that are excuses to give us a minute. The trailer's door is open to the garden, and the night draws a shadowy breath.

Sawyer rests his hands on the back of a chair, fingers flexing on the carved wood. "Tomorrow we pull our hardware and let Nathan's team stand the line."

"Right." The word is a smooth stone, and I turn it in my mouth. "Thank you."

He shakes his head once. "Don't thank me for doing the thing I promised."

I shift my weight. The floorboard squeaks—a stupid human noise in a house that's held too much not-human lately. "You don't want to leave."

"No." He doesn't paint it pretty.

"And I'm not ready for you to stay. Not the way it was." That hurts to say. It's the only honest thing. "I keep seeing doorways when I close my eyes."

"I know," he whispers, and I believe him.

"I want…" My throat tightens around the truth. "I want the next thing we build not to be on top of a crater. I want a kitchen table stained on purpose. I want to invite you in without the word *guard* in the air."

He is very still. "Tell me what you need."

"Time," I say. "And… proof. Not from you—" I shake my head quickly when something in his face flickers. "From the world. That it can go a week without trying to eat us."

"It can try," he says, mouth curving. "We've gotten very good at making it fail."

I laugh once, a tiny, cracked thing. "Stay in the city awhile? Not in this house, not in that hallway. Be reachable. Drink coffee like a civilian. Text me photos of boring things. Let me miss you in a way that isn't breathing through duct tape."

His eyes go soft at the corners. "I can do that."

"Good." I reach out—briefly, brave—and brush my fingers over his knuckles where they grip the chair. A current arcs. He could trap my hand, but he doesn't. "Tell me when the hearing dates are. I want to stand at the back of the room."

"You won't have to stand alone."

"I know." I look up at him, and then down at our nearly-not-touching hands. "Don't go too far."

"Never," he says, that private vow tone that bends something inside me into a shape that fits my ribs again.

The next day is all cables and cases and the sound of things unlatching. The BRAVO trailer folds its silver mouth; Rae wraps up cords with the satisfaction of a job done mercilessly well. Riggs hugs Vanessa—who pretends she doesn't like it and then doesn't let go for ten seconds too long. He clasps Edgar like they're old friends headed back to the same war. Anderssen scratches the K-9 he's borrowed one last time under the collar. Our house, which had learned the BRAVO heartbeat, quiets.

Nathan's agents take their posts. Their polos look almost cheerful. They wave at me like neighbors. I wave back. The world shrinks to the normal size of a wealthy family with a bad month, and it feels almost obscene and exactly right.

Sawyer does one more perimeter walk at dusk, not because he needs to but because leaving without it would feel like leaving a door open. I join him halfway, under the wisteria that smelled like honey the night I let him into my bed for the first time. The scent tonight is sharper, as if the vine has learned a lesson about sweetness and edges.

We walk without touching, our arms almost brushing, his stride shortened to match mine without letting me pretend it's not because of the deep bruise blooming over my hip.

At the south garden gate, we stop. The cut grass where the van idled looks like nothing, a patch that could be anywhere. My stomach rolls anyway.

"I hate this patch of earth," I say.

"I know," he murmurs. He looks at the gate the way he looks at blueprints—scanning, calculating. "Nathan's team will shift the camera, add a beam here, refocus sightline. But we can give it a better story too."

Sawyer

He crouches suddenly, frowning at the hedge. I catch a glint of metal where the dirt meets the stone: the broken tail of the zip tie Rae didn't find because the wind pushed it under. He picks it up, holds it on his palm like a cursed wishbone.

"Want me to trash it?" he asks.

I shake my head. "No." I take it, wrap it in a square of blue shop towel from his pocket, and slip it into my jeans. He raises a brow.

"Paint," I say.

After dinner, I go to the studio. Sawyer watches from the doorway awhile, then leaves me to it. I staple fresh canvas, pull a cobalt line across the bottom just where the floor would be in the van, and then I glue the zip tie scrap into the paint, burying it in blue until it looks like it's swimming up instead of dragging down. I add the white line last, thinner than breath, ghosting through, not covering anything, just insisting on a different path.

When it dries, I lift it off the easel and carry it out to the veranda. Night has dressed the garden in navy. The house lights pool warm at my bare feet. Sawyer is there, on the steps, forearms on his knees, profile cut from quiet.

I set the canvas beside him. He studies it a long time, not asking what it means, because he never asks when it's written in paint.

"Name?" he asks finally.

"'Never Cover,'" I say. "For the part of me that thought color could hide blood. It can't. But it can make a map."

He nods, then tips his head toward the thin white thread. "And that?"

"That's the way through."

We sit together in the hush that lives between thunder and the next storm. Down on the street, a paparazzi van idles and then gives up, moving on for lack of spectacle. A night bird claims the oak. Edgar laughs at something in the kitchen, and Nathan's radio crackles low near the front door. The world keeps making small, normal noises. I let them in.

Finally, Sawyer stands. "We roll at oh-nine," he says, almost apologetic. "Dean's got a training block in Atlanta he'll pretend I asked for." He scrubs a hand over the back of his neck. "I'll be twenty minutes away by plane. Forty-five by reckless driving. Two seconds by text."

"Send pictures," I say, chin up. "Of boring things."

He smiles, the kind that breaks and mends me in one motion. "Copy."

He bends—slow, accounting for how air works now—and presses a kiss to my hair. Not my mouth. Not yet. It lands like a promise placed on a shelf where I can see it and decide when to take it down.

Sawyer

"Goodnight, Cam," he murmurs.

"Goodnight, Soldier Boy," I answer, the words a little steadier every time I say them.

In the morning, the BRAVO convoy pulls away. Rae leans out the passenger window to wolf-whistle, and Riggs salutes two-fingered. Anderssen honks exactly once because any more would make it a parade. Sawyer takes the driver's seat of the last SUV. He doesn't look back right away. He looks forward, checks his mirror, looks left, right, like always. Then he finds me on the steps, lifts two fingers from the wheel. *You okay?* the gesture says.

I lift my hand, hold his gaze. *Go. I'm okay.*

He mouths *text me* and pulls through the gates. Nathan's agents shift in to fill the space like they've practiced it their whole lives. The street swallows the taillights.

The house breathes. So do I.

I go to the studio and set a small canvas on the easel—just big enough for a postcard. I paint a coffee cup in black and white, a smudge where steam would be, and a crooked little slice of sky in blue. I snap a picture and send it to a number I didn't know by heart two months ago and now could dial in the dark.

Me: *Boring thing #1.*

The dots appear instantly. **Sawyer:** *Most beautiful coffee I've ever seen.*

I smile. The bruise on my hip aches and then, after a beat, doesn't.

Tomorrow there will be hearings and statements and reporters who try to pry narrative out of me like a rock with a chisel. There will be my father in a suit that doesn't fit right because shame has its own tailor, and there will be children at a wall with paint under their nails showing me ten new ways to turn blue into breath. There will be Nathan's agents walking their quiet beats. There will be my phone, buzzing at sane hours with photos of parking lots and paper receipts and Sawyer's boots and a Texas sky.

And when I'm ready, there will be a door opening that doesn't creak like a warning, and a man stepping over the threshold not because he's paid to guard my life, but because I asked.

For now, I rinse my brushes, hang my apron, and leave the studio light on low. It turns the white line on the new canvas into a moonlit river across blue, the zip tie hidden underneath like a fossil from a time when I didn't know what I could survive. I stand a minute and let the sight write itself on the inside of my eyes.

Color can't cover blood.

But it can point the way home.

25

Sawyer

Three weeks, four court dates, and more coffee than a platoon in winter. That's how long I give her the quiet she asked for. It's how long I keep one foot out of the house and both eyes locked on it, working the case to the nub while letting space do its gentler work. We close loops: Vale folds, pleads to conspiracy and manipulation, agrees to testify against the black-listed fixer; Kestrel dissolves in a cloud of statements; Rourke learns he's not half as dangerous in a jumpsuit under lights as he was in a mask. Gregory sits under oath and under the weight of what he did. He's smaller, but he doesn't look away. HarborShield settles into their rotation, unobtrusive, competent. The city exhales.

And me? I live in a rental in Atlantic Heights that still smells like paint, run drills with BRAVO Team, file after-action reports, and try to teach my body that every midnight creak isn't a van door finding us again. I tell myself space is part of the mission. Sometimes that feels noble. Sometimes it feels like standing at parade rest outside a room where your whole life is sleeping.

On a Thursday that glows like hammered copper, my phone buzzes with a photo. A crooked mug, a curl of steam painted as a smudge, a strip of sky dashed in blue above it. **Boring thing #12**, the caption reads.

I don't even realize I'm smiling until the mirror tells me. My thumbs move. **Permission to trade boring for better?** I send.

Dots. Then: **Tonight. Seven. Gate code unchanged.** A pause long enough to make me lean against the kitchen counter. **Bring nothing but you.**

I stand in my rental and let that settle into my bones. Then I shave like a rookie on inspection day, iron a shirt that's never seen a crease, and try not to count miles between hearts like yards between blast craters.

NATHAN IS on the veranda when I pull through the gates. He lifts a hand. "We'll keep the perimeter light and the porch lighter," he says, reading my face the way all good guards read a client's weather. "Go on in, Maddox."

"Thanks for holding the line," I tell him, because gratitude belongs in the open.

Inside, the house isn't a fortress tonight. It's a home. Lamps set low, windows cracked to let the jasmine ride in. Somewhere Edgar hums—old soul song turned soft. The white line she painted months ago—*Never Cover*—hangs in the entry, thin as breath, bright as oath.

She waits for me at the base of the stairs.

Blue dress, barefoot. Paint on her fingers like she forgot to finish washing it off. Hair down, eyes the color that started this whole war in my chest. For a second we don't move; we just drink each other in, re-memorize edges dulled by distance.

"Hey, Soldier Boy," she says, like a secret we share.

"Hey, Blue," I say, because that's what she is to me—color and oxygen.

We close distance without thinking. She stops with her fingers at my shirt placket, not touching yet. "I'm okay," she says. "I needed time, and you gave it. I needed proof, and the world handed some over. I needed to know that this next part belongs to us and not to the fear that barged in. I know now."

My hands find her waist with care born from a thousand don'ts and one resounding do. "What do you want?" I ask, because consent is music and I can't hear enough of it.

"You," she says simply. "In this house, in my studio, in my mornings. Not as a line item on a security plan but as the reason the kettle whistles."

I swallow, and it lands like something holy. "Copy," I whisper, and then she's in my arms.

The first kiss is careful—like we're fitting a hinge back into a door. The second forgets about carpentry and remembers fire. She takes the collar of my shirt in both hands, pulls, and I go willingly, letting her set the pace. Months of sleeping on chairs and walking perimeters and staring at ceilings slip off my spine when she opens against me, when her breath sighs my name in a way that rewires a soldier down to boy.

"Upstairs," she breathes, tugging my hand. I nod and follow, not because I don't know the way but because being led by her has become my favorite kind of map.

Her suite is different tonight—candles low, the bed new with indigo linen. On the dresser there's a small canvas leaning on the mirror: a zip-tie scrap buried in blue, a white line cleaving through like a trail you can trust. She sees my eyes land, nods once. "I wanted that patch of earth to learn a better story," she whispers.

"It did," I say, stepping close again. "We did."

I kiss her like that's a fact we both can live in.

Sawyer

Heat rises, slow, uncoiling. She slides my jacket off, folds it with an absent grace that makes me stupidly hungry. My fingers learn the back of her dress where the zipper hides; I move slow, giving her time to reconsider, to laugh, to stop me. She doesn't. The fabric whispers down, and she's standing in soft lace and bravery. I keep my eyes on hers as long as I can, then let my gaze travel with reverence that's half prayer.

"Beautiful," I say, because my vocabulary is battlefield blunt and this is the only word that lands anywhere close.

She steps into me, presses a kiss under my jaw, fingers slipping beneath my shirt. "Show me," she says.

I do what she asks, unbuttoning slow enough to make my own hands shake. Her palms touch my chest like they're learning terrain she intends to paint later. I feel more seen than stripped. When my shirt hits the floor, she tips her head, studies a scar like a curator and a lover at once, and presses her mouth to it. I forget how to breathe correctly for a second. She smiles against me, small and wicked.

We make it to the bed in a series of stumbles and laughter and quick, sharp inhalations when fingers find warm skin. I lie back, and she follows, braced above me, hair slipping around us like a curtain that keeps the world out. "I want to set the pace," she says, breathless but sure. "But you can take the wheel whenever you want."

My grin is helpless. "Shared command," I murmur. "My favorite kind."

Her mouth traces the geography of me—the line of throat and shoulder and the places no one sees except the few who've earned maps. I return the cartography, fingers sketching a path down her spine; my palms span her hip, learn its new shapes—strength and a bruise flowered into yellow and green. She shivers when I mouth the edge of lace. I slow, and check her eyes. She nods, a yes that's both small and blazing. The lace joins the growing trail on the floor.

We take our time because we can. We've earned a clock that doesn't tick like a bomb. She rides me down into the mattress with a gasp that's all light after the tunnel. I meet her there, hands guiding, hearts synced. The world narrows to breath and skin and the long, rolling rhythm you make when you know you're not stealing minutes, you're spending them like a currency that keeps printing.

"Look at me," she whispers as the crest builds, and I do—God, I do—until the room blurs at the edges, until her mouth opens into my name, until the only thing I know is that love feels like coming home in a body that knows the route by heart.

After, we don't rush the return. She collapses on my chest, cheek over my heartbeat. I smooth her hair back and kiss the spot where protest and praise share a language. The ceiling is the same as it always was, but the

Sawyer

air under it is different—cleaner, like the house exhaled with us.

"I want to say something ridiculous," she says after a while, voice muffled in my skin.

"Please do," I say. "Ridiculous is my favorite genre lately."

She lifts her head. Her eyes are still starry and a little wet at the corners. "Move in with me," she says, like a dare and a prayer at once. "Not tomorrow. Not in a way that drags your duffel by the strap and calls it commitment. After the sentencing. After my father's board finishes building the scaffolding around what's left. When the kids finish the second half of the mural and the city looks a shade kinder. Move in then. Bring your stupid kettlebell and the pan you claim is iron but is definitely not. Bring the ugly mug you refuse to throw out. Bring the way you look at me like I'm what happens after a war ends."

There are a lot of things I can do under fire. Talking is not always one of them. I manage to prop up on an elbow, frame her face with my other hand, and find my voice. "Copy," I say, hoarse and happy and every other thing. "And while we're swapping ridiculous…" I lean down, fish the small box I stashed in my discarded jacket, and hold it out. Her eyes widen, equal parts shock and oh-God-no-you-didn't and yes-yes-you-did.

"Don't panic," I say fast. "This isn't an ambush. It's an idea I've been carrying around like a coin. You don't have to cash it yet." I flip the lid. Inside, a simple band—brushed platinum, thin as the white line she painted, inlaid across the center. "I asked a jeweler to make a line that would never rub off. When you're ready. Not because I need to stake a claim. Because I want to build the rest of the map with you."

Her hand flies to her mouth, and laughter bubbles up, the kind people make when the universe gets it right for a change. "You carried a ring in your pocket while you patrolled my hallway?"

"And in three safe houses and one command trailer," I admit, sheepish and not. "I almost asked you when I was prying a flash-bang out from under a rolling door. Thought better of it."

She sits, tucks her legs under her, and takes the band out carefully like it might be thin glass. She balances it on her finger without sliding it home. "After the sentencing," she says, voice warm and steady. "After the mural. After we let the world stop screaming for at least three consecutive weeks. Then—yes. Put that on me."

My grin is a stupid thing with teeth. "Then it's a plan."

We make love again because saying yes to a future makes you greedy for the present. It's slower this time, softer, a study in the way heat can be a kind of prayer and not just a flare. We learn each other again with the silly, sweet joy of people who didn't just survive the fire—they built a hearth out of what didn't burn.

Sometime in the dark hours, the house creaks the way old houses do when the night settles deeper. She stiffens and then remembers where she is, who she's with. I run my palm down her arm, count out my four by fours in her ear—breathe with me—and she melts again, sleep sneaking in like a kind thief.

WEEKS TURN LIKE GOOD PAGES. The sentencing lands with numbers that feel like justice measured instead of rage vented. The kids finish the mural in a crush of color that makes old men cry on a corner where nobody used to stop. Gregory shows up only when invited, listening more than talking, building a scholarship that doesn't have his name on it. HarborShield becomes part of the house, like Edgar and the wisteria and the way the afternoon light finds the stairwell and turns it gold for seven minutes each day.

I move in like a soldier unlearning how to live out of bags: one drawer, then two; a mug that she calls hideous and then uses; a kettlebell that Edgar threatens to dust. With Dean's blessing I take fewer long-haul details and more local contracts that let me wake up with her hair on my ribs and the sun thinking about climbing over the ridge. BRAVO becomes a hummingbird in the background instead of the engine under every step. It's weird. It's good.

One evening in early fall when the city smells like fog and baked brick, Cam and I take the long way home along the Boardwalk. She buys a paper cone of candied almonds and makes me hold it until my fingers stick. When we reach the studio, she climbs the steps two at a time and stops under the skylight, breathless for no reason that has to be solved.

"Ready?" she asks, mischief and courage braided.

"For what?"

"For a door that doesn't creak." She takes the ring out of the pocket where she's kept it like a talisman between then and now. The studio light finds the inlay and turns it into a thread of moon. She holds it to me.

I take it like ammunition and prayer. "Camille Kingsley," I say, because full names make good vows, "you are color and oxygen and the bravest person I've ever met. Be my home, and I'll be yours. Not as a wall you hide behind but as the roof we choose to build together where rain sounds like music."

She laughs, chokes, nods. "That was… very Sawyer."

"I do my best work unscripted," I murmur, and slide the band onto her finger. It fits like it was made for her.

It definitely fucking was.

She kisses me there under the skylight, almond-sweet and salt-wet and yes. Later we tell Vanessa, and she screams so

Sawyer

loud HarborShield checks the cameras. Later we tell Dean, and he says "about time" and sends a bottle of something old enough to vote. Later we tell Gregory, and he cries like a man and not like a CEO.

We don't plan a big thing. We plan a right one. Friends, kids from the mural, a courthouse judge who owes Hartley a favor, and our hands blue with a bit of paint because she swore she wouldn't scrub it all off for anybody's photos. I wear a suit that had to be talked into being a suit; she wears a dress that looks like someone painted the twilight on silk and draped it over bones and breath. The ring catches the sun and throws a line across her palm, and for a second it does look like a door where there wasn't one before.

That night, when the last of the laughter slides down the hall and the house settles around us like a big, content animal, she pulls me to the floor of the studio and we make a mess with intent—paint under nails, color on shoulders, my shirt sacrificed to art again. We fall asleep on drop cloths, and I wake with her hair in my mouth and a smear of cobalt on my jaw and the kind of happiness that makes you feel a little dumb and very alive.

In the morning, coffee whistles. Edgar clatters. The wisteria tries to worm its way in through the window like it wants to bless the chaos. I'm barefoot, unarmed except for the knife I keep for bagels, and so stupidly at peace I almost don't recognize myself. Then she walks in wearing my T-shirt and the ring, hair wild, eyes steady.

"Morning, husband," she says, sleep in her voice and a smile I'd kill for if killing were the thing needed.

"Morning, painter of my heart," I say, because ridiculous is still my favorite genre.

We drink from the ugly mug and the pretty one, share the almond cone we didn't finish, and watch the city blink itself awake. Outside, the world does what it always does—aches, mends, tries again. Inside, we do what we learned the hard way—hold, laugh, make it loud when loud is needed, make it quiet everywhere else.

And on the wall by the stairs, the white line glows thin and stubborn through blue, cutting a path like a promise that refuses to fade. It doesn't cover anything. It doesn't need to.

It shows the way home.

Epilogue
SAWYER

Three months after the last gavel fell, Saint Pierce tastes like salt and second chances.

Morning slides in through the studio skylight and finds me exactly where my best days start—wrapped around Cam on the paint-splattered rug, our coffee cooling on the windowsill, the city humming as if it's throat-singing blessings down the block.

Her left hand is flung across my chest, the thin platinum band catching the light like the white line in her painting, a vow that never rubs off. She blinks awake, smiles the kind of smile you can roadtrip by, and lifts her chin for a kiss.

"Good morning, husband," she murmurs, voice warm with sleep.

"Good morning, painter of my forever," I say, because I've earned the right to be ridiculous and she lets me.

The radio on the workbench crackles—Dean's line. I groan, and Cam laughs, shoving at my shoulder.

"Go save the world," she says, "and bring back croissants."

"Yes ma'am." I kiss her nose, then her mouth, then stand and snag a T-shirt. She sits up, tucks her knees under her shirt, and watches me the way people watch sunrises they know won't storm.

Dean doesn't waste syllables. "I've got Riggs in my office pretending he can't hear me. Come calm your favorite berserker."

"On my way."

Cam steals my baseball cap and sets it backward on my head. "Be nice to him," she says. "And text me his grumpy face."

BRAVO'S OFFICE still smells like coffee and gun oil, like competence with a citrus top note. Rae is at her terminal, flipping a pen through her fingers, amused. Riggs is leaning in the doorway to Dean's glass-walled office, arms crossed, beard more mutinous than usual.

Dean looks up when I enter, lifts his brows in that *your turn* way he's perfected.

Sawyer

"What's the emergency," I ask, "besides Riggs scaring the potted plants?"

Riggs grunts. "New assignment."

"Congratulations," I say. "Why do you look like someone glued your boots to the ceiling?"

Dean steeples his fingers. "A high-visibility tour. Four cities, twelve days. Large checks, larger egos, lots of cameras. Our client asked for BRAVO by name."

"Your client," Riggs says, "also asked specifically for *me*." He glares like it's a trap. "And I don't do glitter tours."

"Which client?" I ask, already suspecting.

Rae spins, grin feral. "Vanessa."

The name hits like a thrown match in dry brush. I school my mouth. "Ah."

Riggs scowls harder. "She's chaos in heels."

"You are a human lock," I say. "Could be a match made in safe-cracking."

Dean slides a file across the desk. "Someone's been sending her organization's inbox some creative threats. Mostly noise, one or two notes that got the ADA's attention—timing, insider details about her stops. She's moving a lot of money and attention; that attracts moths and wolves. She trusts us. She trusts you."

"I can protect her," Riggs says, "but I won't babysit a publicity circus."

"Protecting her is the job," Dean says. "Paparazzi are weather. Work around it."

Riggs stares at the carpet like he might chew it. "She talks. A lot."

Rae snorts. "So do you. Usually in three-word sentences."

I rest a hip on Dean's desk. "What's the real rub, brother?"

Riggs meets my eyes. For a second the grizzly flickers and I see the man who held the line with me in places where maps ran out. "She makes fun of me," he admits. "And I… don't hate it."

"Translation," Rae says, "he likes the sunshine but refuses to admit he needs SPF."

Dean slaps the file once. "Flight tomorrow. Your advance pack is done. We already pinged local PDs and did venue sweeps. You'll be primary. Rae's your remote. Don't make me regret splitting you two again."

Riggs takes the folder like it weighs a hundred pounds and a feather. "If she calls me Beard-Mountain in public, I'm going to—"

"—smile," I say, "and move her three inches left to give the camera a better line of sight."

"Go away," he mutters.

I clap his shoulder. "You'll be fine."

"Tell that to my blood pressure." But when he turns, I catch the reluctant spark. The big man likes a challenge. He always has.

As if conjured by complaint, the office door bangs open and Vanessa breezes in trailing citrus perfume and a storm of scarves.

"There he is!" she says, pointing at Riggs as if selecting a prize on a game show. "My favorite monolith. Ready to live on planes and eat mini-pretzels while glaring at millionaires?"

"No," Riggs says, deadpan.

She beams. "Perfect."

Dean's mouth twitches. Rae bites her knuckle. I press my lips together to keep from grinning.

Vanessa spots me, kisses my cheek, then plants a more decorous one on Dean's airspace out of respect for rank. "Cam says you're bringing dessert tonight to celebrate my imminent martyrdom."

"Croissants," I say. "And earplugs for Riggs."

"I don't need earplugs," Riggs rumbles.

She pats his biceps. "You will."

They square off for a heartbeat—her spark to his flint—and then, like a physics trick, both edges soften by a degree. Dean meets my eyes over their heads: *see?* I nod: *Oh, I see.*

When they leave to "discuss itineraries" (Vanessa's phrasing; Riggs's phrasing involves verbs like *assess* and *secure*), Dean leans back and exhales.

"That one's going to be interesting," he says.

"Understatement of the year," Rae mutters.

I text Cam **Grumpy face unlocked** with a stealth photo of Riggs scowling at a color-coded calendar Vanessa has already taken possession of. Cam replies with a heart and a paint emoji. Then: **Dinner at seven? I have a surprise.**

THE SURPRISE IS an outdoor table under the wisteria, Edison bulbs strung low, Edgar's pot roast making the whole block consider crashing. HarborShield nods when we pass; they feel like cousins now, not guards ghosting the edges.

Cam emerges from the kitchen carrying a small cake—pale blue icing, a thin white line piped across the top like a river. My throat gets tight in a way I don't mind.

"Happy 'first day we met without a ticking thing between

us' day," she says. "It's a bit arbitrary, but anniversaries should be about feel, not calendars."

"It's perfect," I tell her, because it is. We slice it, we eat too much, we laugh when frosting streaks her lip and I insist on removing it with my mouth. Sometime between second helpings and leaning back to look at the stars, my phone buzzes with a text from Riggs: **Plane wheels up 0900. If Vanessa drowns me in scarves, bury me with my boots on.** I send him a thumbs-up and a prayer hands, and Cam grins, toasting the sky.

"To the monolith and the hurricane," she says. "May they meet in the middle."

After dinner we dance without music, just sway where we are, her cheek on my chest, my mouth in her hair. The city throws us a breeze; the wisteria throws us a blessing.

"I want kids," she says into my shirt, quiet and certain. "Not tomorrow. Someday. Paint-under-their-nails kids. A dog that sheds on everything. A life that looks like the morning after a good party."

No bomb in the world could make my heartbeat louder. "Copy," I say, voice rough. "We'll teach them knees and noise and how to find the way out of any room."

"And to draw white lines," she adds. "Always."

We move through the house like people who finally believe it won't disappear if they blink. In the studio we stand before *Never Cover* and hold hands without talking. In the stairwell we kiss like the first time and the last time and the thousand in between. In our bedroom, where the window has learned our names, we fold into each other with the easy hunger of two people who remember what it cost to earn this ease.

Heat flares, deep and steady. I lay her back in the blue linen and worship with hands that learned restraint long before they learned joy. She laughs into my mouth when I say something dumb and tender; she answers with a roll of hips that turns vows into fireworks. We take our time because we can, because time finally belongs to us. When we crest, it's not a flood but a tide—inevitable, clean, the kind that leaves shells where rocks used to be. We stay tangled, and afterward I fall asleep with her leg over mine and her hand on my heart like she's the one guarding it now. She is.

MORNING BRINGS croissants and a photo from Riggs of Vanessa asleep in a first-class seat, mouth open, a scarf cocooned like a hurricane in nap form. **I'm doomed,** he captions. Then, after a beat: **She snores cute. Do not tell anyone I said that.**

I show Cam. She smirks and sends back: **Proud of you, Beard-Mountain.** He replies with a middle-finger emoji and a location pin from the tarmac.

Sawyer

Dean pings the group with **Keep heads on a swivel. Orange Team is a call away.** Rae adds **Try the lemon bars at the Charleston stop. Worth a detour.** The feed scrolls with logistics and jokes and the kind of shorthand you only get after bleeding together and making it out.

I step onto the veranda with coffee and watch the sky make up its mind. Cam slips under my arm, chin on my shoulder. Down on the street, a school bus sighs; up the block, a runner huffs past; inside, Edgar sings to himself as he polishes a bowl like it's a trophy.

"We did it," she says, not as a surprise but as a record for our own archive. "We made it through the part where stories try to make themselves out of us."

"We wrote our own instead," I say.

She nods, tips my face toward hers, and kisses me like a chapter end and a chapter start share a line. It's simple. It's everything.

Later we'll go to the mural and touch up a corner the rain tried to eat. Later I'll teach a BRAVO workshop to a bunch of rookies about what to do when the threat isn't just a person but a narrative. Later we'll pick up a leash and meet a shepherd mix at the shelter who will absolutely own this house in two days.

For now we stand, and breathe, and let the world do what it does while we keep doing what we promised—hold the line, draw the way through, make it loud with love and quiet with trust.

Down the coast, a monolith and a hurricane are learning orbit. Here, under wisteria and a sky that finally trusts us, my wife slips her hand into mine and squeezes once—steady, coded, always—and my whole body answers back.

Always.

THANK you so much for reading Sawyer and Camille's story. I had so much fun writing this one, and enjoy bringing these security specialists to life.

Preorder Riggs and Vanessa's story: CLICK HERE!

Want more of the Maddox Team? Head over to my Patreon to check out all the behind-the-scenes, extra epilogues, bonus content including recipe cards from Edgar, Dean's case files, **BRAVO SWOLL** Cookbook, an ALT-POV from Riggs at the mural project. I'll also be sharing Riggs, Book Two over there as well.

CLICK HERE, or visit https://www.patreon.com/loganchance

Riggs and Vanessa are coming soon. I can't wait for you to meet this feisty couple.

Want to read about the Men of Maddox Security? Keep reading for an excerpt from Defending What's Mine, Asher's story.

Also, you can catch up with all the Men of Maddox Security now, all books are now live and free on Kindle Unlimited.

Sneak Peek Defending What's Mine

Asher

I'm cutting it close. It's a rookie mistake. I push through the revolving doors of the downtown Saint Pierce highrise, stepping from blistering asphalt into chilled marble. The temperature drop is a welcome punch. One breath to reset. I straighten my tie, smooth my jacket, and scan the lobby for threats and choke points. It's a habit.

Elevator to thirty. I post against the side panel, tracking every floor ding like a metronome. When the doors part, I move with a purposeful gait, soft heel-strikes, eyes sweeping the corridor. The conference room's ahead. I spot the frosted glass with silhouettes inside the room, already seated. Late is unacceptable, but dead last is better than hovering outside like dead weight, so I slip in and claim the final chair, back to the wall, sightline on the door.

Dean stands at the head. Broad shoulders, suit impeccable, but there's fatigue in the set of his jaw. It tells its own story. Our gazes lock for half a beat; he registers my presence, files it, continues.

"Thanks for being here," he begins. Voice steady with a commanding frequency. "I know the past year hasn't been easy with me searching for Bishop. I'd like to thank all of you for the hand you played in finding him."

He shuffles briefing folders. He's crisp, methodical. I clock the micro-tremor in his left hand: adrenaline hangover, nothing fatal. The table air is chunky with spent tension; these men wore themselves hollow to close that target. I wasn't on the op, but I respect the mileage etched on their faces.

Dean exhales, softer. "Hopefully we can finally have some peace." The room nods as one unit. Professionals.

I stay silent, absorbing. Profiles around the table read like dossiers—eyes alert, posture disciplined, scars visible and otherwise. This is the bench you want when things go sideways. My objective is simple: earn a spot, hold the line, never be the breach.

I catalog the exit routes, the angle of sunlight on the windows, the cadence of each man's breathing. Mission begins long before boots move. And late or not, I'm here now—ready to prove I belong.

Sneak Peek Defending What's Mine

Dean plants his palms on the head-table, the room settling under his command presence. "I know Isabel has been helping a ton and I'm lucky to have such an awesome sister," he says, nodding toward the empty administrative desk. "I have some assignments that need urgent attention, and I wanted to hand out each one personally."

First real rotation since Dean promoted me from training detail. I force my knee to stay still, posture neutral, but adrenaline hums in my veins.

Dean flips the first dossier—blue cover, intel stamp. He slides it to Ranger. "Ranger I'll start with you first. The G20 Summit Meeting is soon, and this is Tory Ann Malser. She's yours to protect."

"This assignment is critical. The G20 Summit attracts a lot of attention, and not all of it good. Your job is to ensure her safety at all times." Dean flicks a fingertip on the file.

"Is she attending the summit?" Ranger asks.

"No, she isn't. Her father is Fredrick Malser, a world-renowned scientist. He'll be a keynote speaker and will have his own personal security watching over him."

"Why not have her own security watch over his daughter?" Ranger asks.

Dean's expression doesn't shift. "Fredrick has received death threats about speaking at the Summit. And he doesn't trust some members of his own security detail. He wants his daughter kept under the radar. We need to ensure her safety without attracting attention."

Dean shifts. "You'll take her to the safe house near the ocean and hold her until the Summit is over."

Ranger nods once, already scanning routes in his head. "Sounds good."

Dean's gaze shifts to Orion. His head's down, doodling kill-boxes in his notebook. Boone taps Orion's chair with a boot heel; Orion sits straighter, eyes sharpening.

"Orion, you've got the daughter of a socialite, Minnie Green. Briar Green," Dean says, sliding the second folder across. "She's got an ex-boyfriend stalking her, and her mother wants security to follow her to-and-from work."

Orion flips the file open, skims photos of Briar in a khaki bird-handler uniform, bright smile. "Ex-boyfriend," he mutters. "Can't I just scare the shit out of him, make him think twice, and call it a day?."

"It's not that simple," Dean answers, tone flat. "We need to ensure she's safe without escalating the situation."

Orion smirks. "It never is."

Laughter ripples, tension relief. Dean closes the assignment ledger, eyes landing on me last. I sit tall, ready.

Dean finishes handing out files. "Lincoln's already got his assignment." I watched Lincoln tuck his dossier under one arm like it weighs nothing. Boone gets the next folder—thick, color-coded blue for stalker detail.

"Boone, here's your assignment." Dean pushes it across the table. "I briefed you on it last week."

Boone cracks it open, low whistle. "Wow. Who's this?"

"Name's Aubree Ryan," Dean answers, tone all business. "And she's got a stalker too. We're still in the dark about the identity, but she needs to get out of Nashville."

Boone nods once. "I'll take her to my cabin nearby. It's remote, secure."

Dean turns to me, a crimson folder in hand. Color means high-profile asset. "Asher, yours is… different."

My pulse bumps, but I keep posture neutral. Another test, maybe.

He slides the file; the name on the tab reads CHARLOTTE LANE. "Her father hired us. You'll pose as her fiancé during a week-long family retreat."

I flip the cover. First photo: Charlotte in a designer cocktail dress, eyes downcast, sadness baked into the pixels. Something twists beneath my sternum.

Dean outlines the intel—arranged-marriage pressure from a business partner's son, potential hostile takeover if the union happens. "Your cover relationship stops that before contracts hit ink."

I nod, absorbing logistics: location, guest list, emergency exfil points.

Dean finishes the briefing with a sweep of his gaze. "I want everyone to know I'm here if you need anything.."

Chairs scrape. Ranger and Boone file out. I start to follow when Dean says, "Asher, hold up."

I drop back into my seat. Door clicks shut behind the last man.

Dean folds his arms, expression softening a notch. "I chose you because you're closest to Charlotte's age. Optics matter. Don't read hesitation into that."

"I don't." And I don't. Dean's never handed me a job he thought I'd botch. "I'm in."

"Good. Mr. Lane's company can't survive that merger. Keep her convinced, keep the family convinced, and keep anyone else from forcing her hand."

"Understood." We shake hands and step into the hallway.

Chaos meets us. Lincoln has Isabel pinned gently—but firmly—against the wall, murmuring something I can't catch. Isabel looks one twitch from drawing blood.

Her gaze darts past Lincoln, locks on Dean. "And you—" she snaps, finger stabbing the air like a knife.

Not my arena. I sidestep, heading for the elevator before the family fireworks detonate.

Sneak Peek Defending What's Mine

With the file under my arm, my mission's crystal-clear:

1. Infiltrate Lane retreat.
2. Sell the fiancé cover.
3. Make sure no one signs Charlotte's life, or her father's company, away.

Next stop: damsel in distress, pseudo-ring on her finger, and one big corporate shark tank. Exactly where I belong.

CLICK HERE to keep reading. Available in Kindle Unlimited.

PATREON

Calling All Romance Lovers!

Ready for exclusive perks, behind-the-scenes access, and swoon-worthy surprises? Join **Logan Chance's Patreon** today!

Here's what you'll get:

• **Bonus Story** – Read fun, and swoony new bonus stories of older characters AND new ones.

• **Weekly Serials**– Every week follow along as a story unfolds.

• **Exclusive Giveaways** – Win books, swag, and more.

• **Bonus Content** – Unreleased scenes, steamy extras, and secrets from your favorite stories.

PATREON

- **Character Interviews** – Get to know Logan's characters like never before.

- **Sneak Peeks** – Be the first to dive into upcoming books and projects.

And that's just the beginning! There's SO MUCH MORE! Logan's Patreon is packed with romance reader delights you won't want to miss. Cookbooks, recipes, workouts (let's see how the Maddox Men stay in shape), BTS, ALT-POVs, Serials, Bonus Scenes, UNCUT Scenes, Spicy Scenes, Character Interviews, and tons more.

Free members receive a PG-13 bonus scene every month, along with sneak peeks of teasers, covers, and so much more.

Sign up now starting at only $3, and get access to all the swoony goodies today!

CLICK HERE, or visit www.patreon.com/loganchance

Your next favorite romance moment is waiting for you.

About the Author

Logan Chance is a USA Today bestselling author who specializes in high-octane romantic suspense with a touch of humor (or more). Known for weaving intense, pulse-pounding plots with sizzling chemistry, Logan's novels captivate readers from the first page. He was nominated for Best Debut Author Goodreads Choice Awards in 2016. He crafts tales filled with steamy romance, gripping twists, and heart-stopping action.

When he's not writing, Logan can often be found watching great movies, devouring his ever-growing TBR pile, or brainstorming his next captivating series. He currently resides in South Florida, where he continues to pen stories that keep readers on the edge of their seats—and always craving more.

Also by Logan Chance

Maddox BRAVO Team

SAWYER

RIGGS

GUNNER

JAXSON

HAYES

Coming Soon, The Pretty Deadly Things, a dark romcom series. (Be sure to check Amazon for preorder info, or join me on Patreon for free)

MAKE THEM BLEED

MAKE THEM CRY

MAKE THEM BEG

MAKE THEM HURT

MAKE THEM OBEY

MAKE THEM PAY

Men of Maddox Security

PROTECTING WHAT'S MINE

SAVING WHAT'S MINE

GUARDING WHAT'S MINE

TAKING WHAT'S MINE

DEFENDING WHAT'S MINE

Preorder Now:

A Very Bumpy Christmas, Melanie's story

Men Of Ruthless Corp.

SOLD TO THE HITMAN (As featured in the hit Netflix Movie: *Hitman* starring Glen Powell)

The Magnolia Ridge Series

DON'T FALL FOR YOUR BEST FRIEND, Paxton and Hartford's Story

DON'T FALL FOR YOUR BROTHER'S BEST FRIEND, Anya and Griffin's Story

DON'T FALL FOR YOUR GRUMPY NEIGHBOR, Shepherd and Felicity's Story

DON'T FALL FOR YOUR FAKE BOYFRIEND, Brock and Willow's Story

DON'T FALL FOR YOUR EX-BOYFRIEND'S BROTHER, Tripp and Millie's Story

DON'T FALL FOR YOUR GRUMPY HUSBAND, Callum and Violet's Story

The Gods Of Saint Pierce

SAY MY NAME

CROSS MY HEART

CLOSE YOUR EYES

ON YOUR KNEES

Magnolia Point

TEMPTING MR. SCROOGE

LATTE BE DESIRED

THE UMPIRE STRIKES BACK

The Taken Series

TAKEN BY MY BEST FRIEND

MARRIED TO MY ENEMY (BOOK ONE)

MARRIED TO MY ENEMY (BOOK TWO)

STOLEN BY THE BOSS

ABDUCTED BY MY FATHER'S BEST FRIEND

CAPTURED BY THE CRIMINAL

Harmony Hills Series

RUIN'S REVENGE

STEP-SANTA

HOLIDAY HIDEOUT

HATED BY MY ROOMMATE

HARD RIDE

The Trifecta Series

HOT VEGAS NIGHTS

DIRTY VEGAS NIGHTS

FILTHY VEGAS NIGHTS

Vampire Romance

Wicked Matrimony: A Vampire Romance

A Never Say Never Novel
NEVER KISS A STRANGER

The Playboy Series
PLAYBOY

HEARTBREAKER

STUCK

LOVE DOCTOR

The Me Series
DATE ME

STUDY ME

SAVE ME

BREAK ME

Sexy Standalones
THE NEWLYFEDS

COLD HEARTED BACHELOR

Holiday Romance Stories
FAKING IT WITH MR. STEELE

A VERY MERRY ALPHA CHRISTMAS COLLECTION

MERRY PUCKING CHRISTMAS

Steamy Duet

THE BOSS DUET

Box Sets

A VERY MERRY ALPHA CHRISTMAS COLLECTION

ME: THE COMPLETE SERIES

FAKE IT BABY ONE MORE TIME

THE TRIFECTA SERIES: COMPLETE BOX SET

THE PLAYBOY COMPLETE COLLECTION

FILTHY ROMANCE COLLECTION

THE TAKEN SERIES BOX SET: BOOKS 1-3

THE TAKEN SERIES BOX SET BOOKS 4-6

Made in the USA
Columbia, SC
03 October 2025